Tangled in His Embrace

By

Sherri Hayes

Tangled in His Embrace
Sherri Hayes

Copyright 2018 by Sherri Hayes
Paperback ISBN: 978-1-948471-99-2

Photo and cover design by Sara Eirew

This is a work of fiction. Names, places, characters and incidents are the product of the author's imagination and are fictitious. Any resemblance to actual persons, living or dead, events or establishments is solely coincidental.

Other Books by Sherri Hayes

Finding Anna series
Slave
Need
Truth
Trust

Daniels Brothers series
Behind Closed Doors
Red Zone
Crossing the Line
What Might Have Been

Serpent's Kiss series
Welcome to Serpent's Kiss
Burning for Her Kiss
One Forbidden Night: A Serpent's Kiss Novella
Longing for His Kiss

Single Titles
Strictly Professional
A Christmas Proposal: A Strictly Professional Novella

Acknowledgments

A special thank you to my beta reader, editor, and proofreaders, who make what is a very painful process for most authors tolerable. My stories wouldn't be as good without you.

Dedication

This book is dedicated to my readers. Thank you for letting me share my imagination with you.

Chapter 1

Gabrielle Lewis peeked inside her daughter's bedroom to check on her. Taylor sat on the floor near her toddler bed, brushing her favorite doll's hair. It took her a moment to realize anyone else was in the room. "Is'bella likes it when I brush her hair."

"Looks like you're doing a great job."

Taylor grinned. "Can I take her with me to Daddy's house?"

Plastering a smile on her face, Gabby swallowed the knot in her throat and answered her daughter. "Of course you can."

"Yay," Taylor said, rising from her spot on the floor and walking over to her box of toys. She took out several items, sorting them into piles. Gabby was sure there was some sort of logic there, but she couldn't say what it was.

"I'll be in the kitchen if you need me."

Her daughter didn't comment as she continued to do whatever it was she was doing with her toys.

Gabby was in the middle of slicing up some carrots when she heard the doorbell ring. Her heart skipped a beat and she almost let the knife slip out of her hands. "Get a grip," she mumbled to herself.

After placing the knife in the sink, she wiped her hands on a towel and went to get the door even though what she wanted to do was hide under her bed and never come out.

Okay, maybe not the bed. Thinking about a bed and Jax together wasn't a great idea.

The doorbell sounded again and Gabby knew she had to suck it up and answer the door. She couldn't leave him standing on her porch all night.

Taking a deep breath, she reached for the knob.

Cool air rushed in from outside, but she barely noticed as she came face-to-face with her daughter's father. Jax Brooks stood on her front porch, staring back at her, as hot as ever. His dark hair, so much like their daughter's, looked as if he'd recently run his fingers through it. And even though it was only three in the afternoon she could see the beginnings of his five-o'clock shadow. Her mouth went dry remembering how that stubble felt against her skin as he kissed his way down her body. Without her permission, her gaze drifted to his lips. Lips that had tasted and explored—

"Hello, Gabby."

She swallowed, trying to push those memories out of her mind, and dragged her gaze up to meet his blue eyes. "Hi."

They stood there for what felt like several minutes but were probably only a few seconds before he cleared his throat. "Can I come in?"

"Oh. Sorry." She moved to the side so he could enter.

He wasn't supposed to affect her like this anymore. She was almost forty, for goodness' sake.

Okay, maybe not forty. She was thirty-six. But close enough. And definitely not anywhere near the jittery eighteen-year-old she felt like.

She closed the door on the cold December air once he was inside even though keeping it open didn't seem like an altogether bad idea. Maybe it would lower her body temperature a little.

Gabby couldn't let her thoughts go down that road again. She needed to put some distance between them. "I'll go get Taylor. She's in her room."

As she started to move away, she felt his fingers wrap around her wrist. His hold wasn't tight. She could have broken it if she wanted, but a part of her didn't want to. A part of her wanted to forget that he'd left them for almost three years. But what she wanted didn't change the facts. She couldn't trust him to stick around. Something she'd learned the hard way.

Jax didn't let go and he didn't say anything. He didn't have to. She felt the connection between them everywhere his skin touched hers.

"Mommy, I can't find—Daddy!" Taylor showed no reluctance as she launched herself across the room toward her father.

The spell broken between them by Taylor's entrance, Jax released Gabby and bent down to gather Taylor in his arms. "There's my little pumpkin."

Taylor giggled. "I's not a pump-kin, Daddy."

"You're not?"

She shook her head.

"How about a snickerdoodle?"

"Uh-uh."

"Hmm." He lifted her in his arms. "What about . . . a raspberry?"

A loud squeal filled the room as he blew raspberries on her stomach.

Watching the two interact caused Gabby's heart to ache. It was obvious Jax loved his daughter, but she'd thought that before. The first time he'd held Taylor in the hospital his face lit up with joy. But that hadn't kept him from taking off two months later.

Taylor was laughing, enjoying the time with her father. As much as Gabby feared what would happen if he left again, she couldn't keep her little girl from him. Or him from her. It wouldn't be right.

"Do you have your overnight bag packed for a weekend at Grandma and Grandpa's?" Jax asked Taylor as her giggling died down. Although Jax had an apartment of his own, he often spent the weekend at his parents' house whenever he had Taylor for the weekend. Gabby wasn't sure if this was more for his benefit or his parents'. They'd visited Taylor periodically over the years, even when Jax was gone, but they'd always seemed to keep their distance most of the time. Gabby wondered if they felt guilty about their son taking off, but she'd never asked. Now that he was back, they'd gone out of their way to spend as much time with Taylor as possible.

"Mommy said I could bring Is'bella."

Jax raised an eyebrow in Gabby's direction.

"Her Aunt Grace brought her a doll back from Chicago."

Before Jax could respond, Taylor was wiggling in his arms, letting him know she wanted to get down. He placed her feet on the floor and a second later she was running down the hall toward her bedroom.

He shook his head and chuckled. "She never stops, does she?"

"Only when she's asleep."

Jax stood in the center of her living room looking as relaxed as ever, while her insides felt as if she'd ridden one too many roller-coasters. How could he be so composed when she was such a mess inside?

"That reminds me," he said, "my parents want to take Taylor to a children's museum in Kansas City. They want to leave Friday and make a weekend of it."

"Okay."

"You're okay with it?"

"Why wouldn't I be?"

He ran his fingers through his hair in a nervous gesture, hinting for the first time that he might not be as calm as he appeared. "I just wanted to make sure. I have to work next Friday, so I can't go and I didn't know if you already had plans—"

"It's fine."

"Are you sure?" he asked.

"It'll give me some time to catch up on my writing."

He nodded. "Thanks."

Since he'd been back, Jax had been ultra-polite. With one exception. Last month she'd gone to pick Taylor up from his place, something she'd done several times before, but their daughter had fallen asleep before she'd arrived. Gabby should have listened to her instincts that night, scooped her daughter up, and headed home immediately. Instead, she'd let him corner her in the hallway and kiss her.

That night she did what she'd promised herself she'd never do again: let a guy get past her defenses. And the worst part was that it was the same guy who had crushed her heart the first time around.

They stood in awkward silence for several minutes before Gabby went in search of Taylor. The sooner she got Jax out of her house the better. She didn't trust herself around him.

"I'm hungry," Taylor whined as they reentered the living room with her coat, her backpack of clothes, and her new doll.

Jax took the backpack from Gabby and knelt down so he could zip up Taylor's coat. "Think you can wait until we get to Grandma's? I'm sure she'll have something you can snack on."

"Cookies?"

"I don't know. We'll have to see when we get there."

She scrunched up her little face, considering this, and nodded. "'Kay."

He smiled at his daughter, and then up at Gabby. "Say goodbye to your mom so we can get going."

Taylor shoved her doll against her father's chest, wanting him to take it, then turned to wrap her arms around Gabby's legs. "Bye, Mommy."

Gabby ran her hand over her daughter's hair, hugged her against her body, and then lifted her up. "You be good for Daddy, okay?"

"I will, Mommy."

She gave Taylor a kiss and handed her off to Jax. Saying goodbye was always the worst part even though Gabby knew she'd see her daughter again in a little over twenty-four hours.

"I'll bring her back tomorrow before dinner."

Gabby held the door open and watched as they left, not caring how cold the air was outside. She blew a kiss to her daughter as they drove away, trying to ignore the conflicting emotions she felt toward the man who, once upon a time, she thought would be her forever.

***

Jackson Brooks tucked Taylor into bed before making his way down the hall to his parents' kitchen. His mom was standing at the sink, doing dishes, and his dad was sitting at the table, shoveling down another piece of cake. Jax went to the cabinet next to the sink and removed a glass.

"Taylor asleep?" his mom asked.

"Not yet." Jax strolled to the refrigerator for some water. Whoever invented the ice and water contraptions on the front of refrigerators was a genius as far as he was concerned. "When I left she was talking to her new doll."

"She's getting so big. I can't believe she's going to be four in a few months."

"You still can't believe this one"—his dad picked up his fork and pointed it in Jax's direction as he responded to his wife's comment—"is old enough to have a kid of his own."

His mom let the water out of the sink and rinsed the suds from her hands. "That's true. It's hard to believe he'll be thirty-eight in March. I still remember the day we brought him home from the hospital."

Jax leaned back in his chair, sipping on his water. How the conversation started varied, but it always ended up in the same place.

"You know, Taylor could use a little brother or sister. I'd love to have a house full of grandchildren."

"It's not that simple, Mom."

"Sure it is. I know you're still in love with Gabby."

"Kathy, leave the boy alone."

"But he loves the girl. Don't tell me you don't see it." His mother stood with her hands on her hips as she addressed his father.

"Of course I do, but it's none of our business." He cut her off before she got a chance to get going again. "He has to do it in his own time. You can't rush him."

His mother huffed. "Fine. I just don't understand why things can't go back to the way they were before. You two were so in love."

"Mom, I walked out and left them for three years. That isn't something Gabby is likely to forget anytime soon."

"Only because—"

"It doesn't matter."

She narrowed her eyes and sent him a look that used to send him running for cover as a kid. "Jackson Theodore Brooks, tell me you've told that poor girl why you disappeared for three years."

Jax arose from the table, downed the rest of his water, and took his glass to the sink. "There hasn't been a good time."

A look of horror crossed his mother's face. "Hasn't bee—"

His father placed a hand on his mother's arm. "Let it go, Kathy. He'll tell her when the time is right."

"Thanks, Dad."

"I didn't say I agreed with you, son, but you're an adult. It's your decision." His father stood to put his empty plate in the sink. "Even if I think it's a bad one."

That night Jax lay in bed for several hours contemplating what his parents had said. Leaving had been one of the hardest things he'd ever done, but at the time he'd felt like it was the best option. Now, seeing the hurt on Gabby's face every time he saw her had him second-guessing his choice.

He was still lying there staring at the celling when he heard his bedroom door being pushed open. Turning his head to look, he saw the silhouette of his daughter framed in the doorway, holding her doll.

Jax sat up in bed. "What are you still doing up?"

She rubbed her eye with the back of her hand. "I looked everywhere but I couldn't find you."

"I'm right here."

Taylor shook her head.

Jax felt as if someone had punched him. He realized she must have been dreaming. "Come here."

She rushed across the room as fast as her little legs would carry her. He lifted the covers, letting her slide in beside him. Taylor snuggled close.

Wrapping his arms around her, he kissed the top of her head. "You had a nightmare. I'm right here."

"But I couldn't find you nowhere. I looked and looked. Even Mommy couldn't find you." He could tell by the sound of her voice that she was on the verge of tears.

"I'm right here and I'm not going anywhere," he said, holding her closer and knowing deep down this was all his fault.

"Promise?"

He cradled her against his chest. "I promise."

A few minutes passed and he thought maybe she'd fallen asleep when he heard her mumble, "Love you, Daddy."

It broke his heart a little more. "I love you, too, Pumpkin."

He fell asleep eventually, although he kept waking up. Taylor was a hotbox and she was plastered against him. No matter how he moved, she would shift her weight so her body was flush against his. By the time the sun was shining through the window the next morning, he felt as if he'd slept under an electric blanket that had been turned up to high all night.

Badly in need of some air and a shower, Jax eased his way out from under his daughter. Once he'd thought she'd woken up, but she rolled over and went back to sleep. He breathed a sigh of relief.

Jax grabbed some clean clothes from his overnight bag and headed down the hall to the bathroom. The room hadn't changed much since he was a kid. There was a new soap dispenser and the shower curtain was different, but most everything else was still the same . . . even the wallpaper.

The water felt good on his overheated skin, but it didn't wash away the guilt Taylor's words from last night had left gnawing in his gut. He'd caused that fear in her eyes, whether he'd intended to or not.

After finishing his shower, Jax looked in on Taylor before making his way to the kitchen. His parents were nowhere in sight, but there was a full pot of coffee sitting on the counter waiting for him. He poured himself a cup and reached for the Sunday paper that had been left sitting on the table. No doubt his mother had already been through it looking for coupons.

"Don't know why you're bothering to read that. It's straight up depressing." His dad strolled into the room and went straight for the coffee. Like father, like son.

"Something to do." Jax sat down at the table and took a drink of his coffee. "Where's Mom?"

"She had to run to the store. We're out of eggs or something." His dad brought his coffee over to the table and lowered himself into the chair across from Jax. "Taylor still sleeping?"

Jax nodded. "Still out like a light."

"I noticed she was in your bed this morning."

"She had a nightmare."

His father didn't try to further the conversation, so Jax focused on the newspaper in front of him.

They sat in silence for several minutes before he couldn't take it anymore. Jax needed a sounding board and his dad was about the only person he could really talk to about this. "Taylor dreamed I had disappeared."

"I see."

"I didn't think she would have been so affected by my absence, given how young she is. I mean she was a baby when I left. She didn't even remember me when I came back," Jax said.

His dad shrugged. "I'm not sure that matters. You were gone. In her eyes, you could just as easily not be there again."

Jax shook his head. "I'm not sure I could do it again. It was hard enough the first time."

"And yet you did it."

"You know why I left."

"I do." Nate Brooks took a sip of his coffee. "Doesn't mean I agreed with your decision. It's like I told you last night. You're an adult. You have to live with your decisions . . . and their consequences."

Jax could still recall that fateful day when he'd gotten the call that had changed the course of his life. He'd gone back and forth over what to do before finally coming to a decision. Taylor was only two months old at the time. She and Gabby had been his life, his future, but in an instant, all of his hopes and dreams were being threatened. "I did what I thought was best."

"For who? You?"

"For Gabby and Taylor," Jax said.

His father lowered his mug and met Jax's gaze. "And you don't think Gabby should have had a say?"

"She would have tried to convince me to stay."

"Maybe. Maybe not. But now you'll never know, will you?"

Jax didn't get a chance to respond. The sound of little feet told him they wouldn't be alone for long, and this wasn't the type of conversation they could have in front of a three-year-old. It did, however, give him a lot to think about. Had he made the wrong decision back then? Was he making the wrong decision now?

He didn't know the answer to that. All he knew was at the time he'd done the only thing he felt he could, which was to leave. He hadn't wanted to be a burden on Gabby. She had their daughter to take care of. She didn't need to be worrying about him on top of it.

But where did that leave him?

He honestly didn't know.

Chapter 2

Gabby spent Saturday evening working on her latest novel. As Taylor got older, it became harder and harder to write. It was easy when her daughter was little, but once Taylor started crawling and walking around things had become a little more challenging. The other day Taylor had run up to Gabby's laptop and tried to read over her shoulder. Granted, Taylor couldn't read all that much yet, but that wouldn't be the case in a few years. That meant Gabby had to wait until her daughter went to bed in order to find time to write. Or, now that Jax was back, for the weekends she was with him.

On Sunday morning, Gabby spent some time tidying up the house before heading over to her mom's. Her sister, Grace, was meeting her there and the three of them were going Christmas shopping. Gabby still had quite a few things to get and time was running out. Christmas was only three weeks away.

Grace's car was already parked out front when Gabby pulled up to her mother's house. Her sister had changed a lot in the last two months since she'd met Alexander. She was getting out more, for one thing. Gabby no longer had to bribe Grace to go shopping. In fact, this outing had been her sister's idea.

The muffled voices of her mother and sister greeted Gabby as soon as she walked through the door, and she followed the sound to the back of the house. "I've been doing some research online, trying to find something I think I can pull off."

"What exactly are you trying to pull off?" Gabby asked her sister as she strolled into the room. Her mom was sitting on the bed, putting on her shoes, and Grace was leaning against the far wall, her arms crossed.

Caroline Lewis finished tying her shoe and hurried across the room to give her oldest daughter a hug. "We didn't hear you come in."

Gabby returned her mother's embrace before raising her eyebrow at her sister, letting her know she was still waiting on an answer to her question.

"I want to make a big Italian dinner for Alexander. It's his first Christmas since being discharged and I want it to be special."

"What about your boss?"

Grace looked confused. "Beth?"

"She's good at cooking, right?"

"Beth's more of a baker," Grace said. "I think her fiancé does most of the cooking."

"Well, there you go. Ask him."

"I can't ask Drew." The aghast look on her sister's face was almost comical.

"Why not?" Gabby asked.

Grace opened her mouth, and then closed it again before responding. "I don't know. I'd just feel awkward about it, I guess."

"Well, if you want to cook a nice meal for your man you're gonna have to get over it."

Grace rolled her eyes. "That's easy for you to say."

"It's not a bad idea, Grace," their mother said, getting in on the conversation for the first time.

Sighing, Grace picked her coat up off the bed and draped it over her arm. "I'll think about it, okay?"

Gabby didn't get a chance to respond before her mother went into herding mode. "Let me get my coat and we can get out of here. I'm starving and I still have a lot of shopping to do."

Three hours later Gabby and Grace were weaving through racks of clothes. Their mom had made a beeline for the bathrooms as soon as they'd entered the store, and so far she'd been MIA.

"Is Alexander all moved in yet?" Gabby asked as she held up a shirt for inspection.

The sides of her sister's mouth turned up slightly in a girlish smile Gabby hadn't seen in a long time, not since Grace found out her husband wasn't coming home from the war. "He was going to bring a couple more boxes over today and that should be it."

"If that smile of yours is any indication, I'm guessing the whole living together thing is going well?"

Grace glanced up at Gabby, and then away. "Yeah."

"Well, I'm happy for you. You deserve it."

Her sister bit her lower lip and averted her gaze to a dress on the rack next to her. "What about you? How are things between you and Jax? I mean . . . have you two . . ."

Gabby knew what her sister was asking. "No. I haven't slept with him again." When Grace remained quiet, Gabby knew she had to say something else. She hadn't meant to make it sound as if Grace shouldn't have asked. Gabby had confided in her sister about it, after all. "It's made things between us more complicated. As if they weren't already complicated enough before."

"So what are you going to do?"

"I have no idea." That was the crux of the issue. What her heart and body wanted weren't in line with what her mind knew she should do. But this wasn't the time to get into all the complexities of her relationship, or lack thereof, with Jax. Gabby could see their mom heading toward them and knew she needed to end the conversation. "I'll figure something out."

"Sorry I took so long," their mother said. "I ran into Maggie as I was coming out of the bathroom. You remember Maggie, right? Her husband, Bret, used to work with your dad."

"How's she doing?" Grace asked.

"He retired last month and they're moving to Arizona in the spring to be close to their grandchildren." As quickly as she'd started the conversation, their mother switched gears. "Speaking of, I saw the cutest pair of shoes. I want to see if you girls like them. I think they'll look adorable with the outfit I got for Taylor."

With a new objective set, Gabby placed the shirt she'd been looking at back on the rack and they all headed over to the kids' shoe section.

By the time they called it a day and arrived back at their mom's house, Gabby's feet and legs felt as if they were about ready to fall off. They'd hit twelve stores in less than five hours. It had been a long time since she'd been on her feet for that long. The good news was that she was officially done with her Christmas shopping. Now all she had to do was drag it home and wrap it all. The thought brought a new sense of dread.

Grace handed her the last of Gabby's bags and she placed it in the trunk of her car before closing it. "Thanks."

"You're welcome." Her sister shifted her weight and Gabby knew something was coming. Probably something she wasn't going to like.

When Grace continued to hesitate, Gabby sighed. "Just spit it out already."

"I know you probably don't want to hear this, but you and Jax need to talk this out."

"There's nothing to talk about. We had sex. It was a mistake. End of story."

"I don't believe that and neither do you," Grace said.

"It doesn't matter." Gabby walked to the other side of the car and opened the driver's side door. "I'm not going there again."

Grace nodded. "I understand. He hurt you."

"I'm over it."

"Are you?"

Maybe this new side of her sister wasn't as great as Gabby first thought. Grace used to let things go. Or maybe that was wishful thinking. Maybe it was more that Gabby really wanted her sister to forget about it. "I have to be. He's Taylor's father and she deserves to have him in her life. I won't deny her that."

"Okay. I get that you don't want to talk about it. But if you change your mind, I'm here."

"Thanks." Before Grace could come up with another angle of questioning, Gabby said her goodbyes and ducked behind the wheel, waving to her sister as she drove away.

It was close to seven by the time she pulled into her driveway and Jax would be bringing Taylor home soon.

Gabby was placing the last of the shopping bags into the back of her closet when she heard the doorbell ring. She made sure everything was hidden, and then went to answer the door.

The cool outside air rushed into her home, followed quickly by a streak of red that was her daughter, who made a beeline for her bedroom with no more than a "Hi, Mommy" and left the sound of giggles in her wake.

Jax stepped inside, chuckling. "I think maybe she had a bit too much sugar this afternoon."

Not wanting to keep the door open, Gabby had no choice but to close it, leaving her standing in her living room alone with Jax. "What all did you give her?"

"We made Christmas cookies today and I think she ate more than she made. Luckily Mom had an apron for her to wear or else her clothes would have been covered in cookie dough." His face lit up as he talked about spending the day with his daughter. It tugged at Gabby's heart strings, bringing up a bunch of feelings she didn't want.

"I'm sure she'll settle down in an hour or so."

He smiled. "Probably."

***

A lock of Gabby's blond hair had fallen out of her ponytail, her loose curls tickling the side of her face every time she moved. The urge to brush it back out of the way was strong, but he resisted. Jax knew it wouldn't stop there. He'd want more. Like he'd wanted more the last time he'd stepped into her personal space to pick a piece of lint from her jacket.

It had been completely innocent, until he'd touched her, felt the heat coming off her body, calling to him. He'd looked into her eyes and in that moment he saw the same need reflected there that he felt deep in his soul. Instinct had taken over and before he knew it she was lying naked beneath him and he was buried inside her.

Gabby tucked the hair behind her ear, drawing his attention back to the present. "Are your parents going to pick her up next weekend or . . ."

"Yeah. Mom was hoping to pick her up from the babysitters so they can beat the Friday rush."

"I'll let Emily know."

There was awkwardness in the air that never used to be there between him and Gabby, and he had no idea how to fix it. After Taylor's nightmare the night before, he didn't know if he deserved for it to be fixed. He'd caused his little girl pain. He deserved to suffer. "I should get going."

A look of relief showed on Gabby's face and it was like a knife to his heart.

"Mommy, why don't we have a Twist-mas tree like Grandma and Grandpa?" Taylor walked into the room, dragging her favorite stuffed animal behind her.

"I just haven't had time to drag everything out of the attic yet." Gabby ran her hand over the top of their daughter's hair in a loving gesture. "Maybe we can do it this week before you leave on your trip with Grandma and Grandpa."

"I can get everything down out of the attic for you if you want," Jax said.

"That's okay. I can—"

"Come on, Daddy. I'll shows you." Before Gabby could even get her refusal out of her mouth, Taylor took him by the hand and coaxed him to follow her down the hallway.

Jax shrugged as he let his daughter lead him down the hall to where the attic access was in the ceiling. He reached up to pull the rope that would lower the staircase. "I need you to stand back."

Taylor moved closer to her mother, one arm wrapped around Gabby's legs.

The fold-up ladder creaked as he lowered it. He looked over his shoulder at Gabby. "Is there still a light up there?"

"Yeah. As soon as you get to the top it'll be on your left."

Jax nodded and climbed the steep rung of stairs leading up to the attic.

He'd only been in Gabby's attic once before. They were fixing up the room that would become Taylor's nursery. It had been a happy time for both him and Gabby. He'd been so full of nervous excitement that he hadn't paid much attention to the attic itself or what was up there.

Gabby's house wasn't all that big, but it still took him several minutes to locate the artificial tree and two boxes of Christmas decorations mixed in with several boxes of toys and baby clothes. He couldn't help but wonder why Gabby was holding on to Taylor's old clothes. Was she hoping to have another baby one day? Or maybe she was holding on to them for her sister.

As much as it shouldn't matter what her reasoning for keeping Taylor's baby clothes was, Jax couldn't shake it off. He carried the boxes Gabby needed down the ladder and placed them along the wall.

Once everything was down, he folded the ladder back up and made sure the access panel was secure before grabbing one of the boxes from where he'd left it. "Did you want these in the living room?"

"I can get them."

He met her gaze and held it for a long moment. "I'm here. Let me help."

She didn't answer right away, seeming to weigh her options. Finally, she nodded. "Yes. Thank you."

Jax didn't stay long after putting the boxes in her living room. It was getting late and he knew Gabby would want to start getting Taylor ready for bed. As much as he wanted to stay, he knew he had given up that right when he'd decided to leave them. He had to be content with the fact that he got to see them both on a regular basis.

The ache in his chest grew as he drove away from Gabby and Taylor toward his apartment a few miles away. It wasn't anything fancy, but that wasn't why he'd picked it. He'd wanted to be near Gabby and his daughter in case they needed him.

He came through his front door, flipped on the hall light, and dropped his keys on the counter. After spending the last two days with Taylor, his place was really quiet. He grabbed a glass from the cabinet, filled it with water, and strolled into the living room to see what was on television.

After surfing through the channels, he found an old movie he hadn't seen in a while. It was full of action, which he was hoping would be a good distraction.

An hour later, he realized it wasn't. His thoughts kept drifting back to Gabby. Well, Gabby and the conversation he'd had that morning with his dad. He knew he needed to tell her where he'd been for the first three years of their daughter's life—why he'd left—but he had no idea how. And truth be told, he was afraid of how she would react. Gabby was a bit unpredictable, but that was one of the things he loved about her. She was also stubborn, which was how he'd known that if he'd told her back then she would have altered her life to stay by his side and support him. He couldn't let her do that.

Jax drained the last of the water from his glass, turned off the television, and headed to his bedroom. Stripping out of his clothes, he ambled into the bathroom to take care of business and brush his teeth before climbing into his bed.

As he lay there with his arms folded beneath his head, he thought over his options. If he and Gabby were going to talk they were going to need to do it without Taylor around. This was too important and the subject matter too serious for a three—almost four—year-old to overhear. It already seemed as if his absence had affected her enough. He didn't want to be the cause of any more nightmares.

With his parents taking Taylor for the weekend, it was the perfect opportunity, but he would need to figure out a way to get Gabby to listen to him. She'd been closed off since he'd returned and even more so since they'd given in to the attraction they still felt for each other. Sweet talking her wasn't going to get his foot in the door.

But maybe honesty would. Gabby didn't like it when people beat around the bush. She preferred direct and honest. He could still remember the end of their first date when he'd walked her to the door, hands sweating, trying to figure out whether or not he should kiss her good night, when she'd surprised the hell out of him by asking if he was going to kiss her already.

The challenge in her eyes had pushed his doubts away. He'd closed the distance between them, cupped the side of her face in the palm of his hand, and pressed his lips to hers. Looking back on it, Jax was pretty sure he started falling in love with her that night.

Thinking about their first date and how Gabby had felt pressed against him had his lower half waking up. He groaned and rolled over to bury his face in his pillow. To say he was sexually frustrated was an understatement. Gabby was the only woman he'd slept with since the night of their first date four and a half years ago. The little taste he'd gotten about a month ago hadn't been enough. Not by a long shot. However, he had no desire to find another woman to satisfy his sexual urges. His body wanted Gabby and so did he.

Jax tried to think of something else, anything else, but it wasn't working. If he thought about work, it brought back the time when Gabby had showed up at his job after hours in the sexiest librarian outfit he'd ever seen.

He hardened at the memory, and Jax knew what he was going to have to do if he had any hope of getting sleep. He snaked his hand into his boxers and grasped the base of his rock-hard cock. As he had many times during the three years he'd been gone, Jax let his thoughts take over as he stroked himself, imagining it was Gabby touching him.

It didn't take long for him to feel the surge of energy shoot up his cock. He gasped, calling Gabby's name as he climaxed. Wishing—hoping—that one day she'd forgive him and it wouldn't only be memories warming him in his bed.

Chapter 3

With Christmas less than three weeks away, Gabby felt as if she were about to lose her mind. She'd had to work late Monday, Tuesday, and Wednesday, which meant she and Taylor hadn't been able to put up the tree and decorations. So when she managed to leave work on time Thursday evening, she knew it would have to be the night even if she was dead on her feet.

After picking Taylor up from the babysitter, she drove home and ordered pizza. She figured that would give them more time to decorate.

"You ready to set up the tree?" Gabby asked.

To her surprise, her daughter didn't seem as excited about it as she thought she'd be. Taylor had asked her at least a dozen times this week if they could decorate the Christmas tree.

Gabby placed the base of the tree down on the couch and went to kneel in front of her little girl. "What's wrong?"

"Daddy's not here." Her lower lip jutted out in a pout.

"You'll see Daddy next weekend when he comes to pick you up."

Taylor's head started shaking. "Daddy has to help put up the Twist-mas tree, Mommy. That's what daddies do."

Gabby felt her chest clench. She thought it would be a few years before Taylor began to question why her mommy and daddy weren't together. Why she had two Christmases. Two birthdays. Two . . . everything. "Some daddies do, that's true. But when mommies and daddies don't live together then sometimes it's the mommies and daughters who decorate the tree."

Her daughter shook her head again. "I want Daddy."

"Your daddy's not here right now, sweetheart, but you can call him on the phone and talk to him if you want." It wasn't a perfect solution, but the offer seemed to calm her down.

Taylor smiled.

Gabby went to get the phone and dialed Jax's number. It rang twice before he answered. "Hello?"

He sounded out of breath and it brought back memories of the last time she'd heard that sound from him. It had the muscles in her belly tightening in anticipation. She'd obviously gone too long since spending some quality time with her vibrator. "Hi. It's me. Gabby."

She heard some noise in the background and a muffled reply from him. "Sorry. I'm just finishing up at the gym. What's up?"

"Taylor wanted to talk to you."

"Sure. Put her on."

Gabby swallowed as she handed the phone to her daughter. Not because she was nervous about Taylor speaking to her father, but rather the image of him at the gym, muscles flexing under the strain of lifting weights . . .

Something poked her leg and she looked down. Taylor had the phone in her hand, using it as a means to get Gabby's attention. "Daddy wants to talk to you."

She took the phone and brought it to her ear. "Hey."

"Hey." He didn't sound as out of breath now, which was good. It made talking to him easier when she wasn't imagining him naked and on top of her. "Taylor asked if I could come help set up your tree. I'm free tonight, so I can come over, but I didn't want to step on your toes."

One glance in her daughter's direction and Gabby knew she didn't really have a choice. If she said no, Taylor's heart would be broken. She was too young to understand the complicated situation. "It's fine. I ordered some pizza. It should be here in about twenty minutes."

"Great. That will give me enough time to grab a quick shower and head over." Gabby heard a door opening and wondered if it was him going into the locker room. She tried to push away the images of him naked in the shower, the warm water cascading over his body. "I'll see you in a few."

Jax disconnected the call, leaving Gabby standing there feeling antsy in a way she hadn't experienced since high school.

"Is Daddy coming?" Taylor asked, practically bouncing up and down at her mother's side.

She put on the best smile she could muster. "Yes. He'll be over in a little while. Now, help me sort out these decorations. Maybe we can get that done before the pizza gets here."

Twenty-five minutes later, Gabby was paying for the pizza while sneaking peeks at the street for any sign of Jax. Despite trying to keep busy while they were waiting on the food to arrive, Gabby had worked herself up into a mess of knots. She wasn't even sure she was going to be able to eat at this point.

"Have a good night," the young man said as he backed away, slipping the tip she'd given him into his pocket.

Gabby was about to close the door when Jax's vehicle pulled up to the curb, sliding in behind the car of the guy who'd delivered their pizza. She stood there frozen as Jax got out of his car, waved to the young man who'd left her doorstep only moments before, and proceeded to make his way up the sidewalk. His hair was slicked back from his recent shower and he looked completely relaxed.

"Sorry I'm late. One of the trainers stopped me on the way out and asked if I could help with her website."

Irrational jealousy surged to the surface as Gabby pictured this unknown woman who most likely didn't need to worry if the extra belly fat from having a child would spill out of her jeans. It was stupid and not what she should be thinking about at that moment. Or ever, for that matter. Jax wasn't hers anymore. He could date anyone he wanted.

"Are you all right?" Jax was frowning.

"Fine." Gabby turned on her heels and marched into the kitchen to get some plates, berating herself the entire way. She needed to get it together. Fast.

"Daddy!"

"Hey, Pumpkin."

Gabby set the table for the three of them, putting a couple of pieces on Taylor's plate before setting the box in the center. She'd ordered a large, thinking they'd have leftovers, but that was before she knew Jax would be joining them. When they were dating she remembered times when he would eat an entire pie himself. Hopefully what they had was enough.

Jax strolled into the kitchen with Taylor in his arms and placed her in her seat. He pulled out the chair next to her and lowered himself down.

"What would you like to drink?" Gabby asked Jax as she handed Taylor a sippy cup full of water.

"Water's fine." He grinned up at her, their gazes locking for a moment before he refocused on his daughter.

Taylor dominated the dinner conversation. She was excited that her father was there, and because she hadn't seen him since Sunday, she had to catch him up on everything she'd done. Gabby had to keep reminding her to eat her food.

Jax helped her clean up, gathering the empty pizza box and napkins and throwing them in the trash while Gabby rinsed the plates and cups and loaded them into the dishwasher. It all felt very normal, comfortable. If only the butterflies that were dancing in her stomach would calm down.

While they were waiting on the pizza to arrive, Gabby and Taylor had opened all the boxes and untangled the lights.

"Hmm. Where should we start?" Jax asked, rubbing his chin as if he was contemplating some great mystery.

Taylor giggled. "With the tree. With the tree."

He hit his forehead with the heel of his hand. "Of course. What was I thinking?"

Gabby shook her head, laughing despite her anxiety. He was so good with Taylor and it was clear to see how much his daughter adored him.

It took them over an hour to put up the tree, decorate it, and set out all the other decorations Gabby had stuffed in the boxes, but by the time they were done her entire house had been transformed. She'd even put up lights along the mirror in the bathroom.

As the evening wore on, Taylor began to slow down. "Time to get your pj's on."

Taylor shook her head even as she tried to rub the sleep out of her eyes. "Not tired."

"Come on, Pumpkin. Let's get you ready for bed and I'll read you a story before I go. How about that?" Jax said.

"Okay." Taylor slid off the couch and took hold of her father's hand before guiding him toward her room.

He sent Gabby a look. She wasn't sure if it was an apology or a look of resignation.

Gabby began gathering the empty boxes and stacking them inside one another. She'd store them in the closet until it was time to take the decorations down. It was easier than dragging them back up into the attic. She was sure Jax would do it for her if she asked, but that wasn't something she wanted to do. The sooner he left her house the better.

***

Jax tucked his daughter in her bed and leaned in to give her a kiss good night.

"Daddy?" Taylor stared up at him with blue eyes so like her mother's.

"Yes?"

"I love you."

A wave of emotion made it hard to swallow. "I love you, too, Pumpkin. Now get some sleep. You have preschool tomorrow."

She rolled onto her side and clamped her eyes closed.

His chest vibrated with a suppressed laugh as he let himself out of her bedroom.

When he emerged from the hallway into the main living space, he found Gabby in the kitchen. She was wiping down the already clean counters. But what did he know? Maybe they really did need washing. "Hey."

He saw her back stiffen before she responded without looking at him. "Thank you for putting her to bed."

"You don't have to thank me. She's my daughter, too."

Gabby kept her back to him and he noticed she'd rubbed the same spot at least a half dozen times.

Closing the distance between them, he placed a hand on her arm, trying to get her attention.

She jumped.

"Sorry."

"It's okay," she said, already beginning to put distance between them.

Jax knew he was going to have to do something to fix things between them. If that meant telling her why he left three years ago then so be it. But not now. Not with Taylor down the hall and able to interrupt them. He didn't want to rush this. It was too important.

Knowing she wouldn't agree to sit down and talk with him about anything other than Taylor, he latched on to his one bargaining chip. "Are you free tomorrow night? Since Taylor will be with my parents, I wanted us to sit down and discuss custody arrangements."

She whipped her head around to look at him, all thought of cleaning seemingly forgotten. "What custody arrangements? You're not . . . I mean . . . I let . . ."

He started to take a step toward her, but stopped himself. "Calm down. I'm not going to try and take Taylor away from you, if that's what you're thinking. I just want to talk about some specifics. Christmas is coming and I want to make sure we're both on the same page, that's all."

"Oh." She visibly relaxed. "Well, we can talk about that now."

"I'd rather do it when we don't have the potential of little ears overhearing."

Gabby looked toward the hallway but, of course, there was no one there. She took a deep breath, squared her shoulders, and lifted her chin. He'd always liked to refer to it as her game face. "Of course. What time?"

"I was thinking around six. I could bring Chinese."

"You don't—"

"Let me buy you dinner. It's the least I can do for interrupting your weekend."

She scraped her teeth over her bottom lip, drawing his attention. He tamped down the urge to rub his thumb over her abused lip and suck it into his mouth.

"Gabby?"

"Okay," she said, barely loud enough for him to hear.

He smiled, trying to lighten the mood. "All right. I'll see you tomorrow night at six." He paused, wanting to say something else but failing to find something that would express what he wanted to say without making her shut down even more than she already was. "Good night, Gabby."

Jax didn't wait for her to say it back. He grabbed his coat and left, reminding himself that waiting to say what he needed to say would be better for both of them in the long run.

***

He spent most of Friday trying to catch up on work. The end of the year was always hectic. All his clients seemed to have a to-do list a mile long and, of course, they wanted it all done before the end of the year.

At one thirty he removed the glasses he used solely for when he had to spend hours staring at a computer screen and rubbed his eyes. Jax had been at it since seven thirty that morning and all the letters and numbers were beginning to blur together. He needed a break.

Leaving his glasses balanced over his keyboard, he padded into his small kitchen and opened the refrigerator. There wasn't a lot there as he hadn't been to the grocery store for almost two weeks. It hadn't seemed necessary when his mom had sent him home with a bunch of leftovers, but those were gone and he was left with not much more than the basics. He was honestly surprised he still had milk that hadn't expired.

Deciding to go in a different direction, he grabbed what was left of the loaf of bread his mom had sent him home with and checked to make sure it was still free of mold before retrieving a can of tuna from the cabinet. It wasn't ideal, but it would fill him up. He had at least three more hours of work to finish before he could call it a day.

Jax didn't realize how hungry he was until he took his first bite. He'd almost devoured the entire sandwich when his cell phone rang. Stuffing the last of it into his mouth, he jogged back over to his desk to see who it was. "Hi, Mom."

"I have someone here who wants to speak to you."

He glanced at the clock on his computer. It wasn't even two yet. "I thought you weren't picking Taylor up until three."

"The news said we're going to get snow tonight and your dad wanted to get there before it starts. He didn't want to deal with all the crazy people on the roads."

While Jax had heard they were going to get some snow, he doubted it would be more than a dusting. St. Louis wasn't exactly known for huge snow falls. But he couldn't blame his dad for not wanting to mess with people who suddenly forgot how to drive at the first sign of snow.

"I want to talk to Daddy." His daughter's voice sounded in the background.

Jax grinned. "Put her on."

His mom chuckled. "Here she is."

"Daddy?"

Tucking the phone between his ear and his shoulder, he rinsed off his plate and set it in the sink. "Hi, Pumpkin. How was preschool?"

That was all his daughter needed to start telling him about her day. Apparently, one of her friends had gotten a hamster and their mom had brought it in for show and tell. "Can I haves a hamster, Daddy?"

Jax could only imagine Gabby's reaction to that. He decided it was probably best to change the subject rather than try to explain to a three-year-old why she wasn't getting a hamster. Although, he figured it could have been worse. He had been only two years older than Taylor when he began begging his parents for a puppy. "We'll have to see. Are you excited about your trip with Grandma and Grandpa?"

And she was off again, this time telling him how she'd introduced his mom to her babysitter. He leaned back against the counter and listened.

It was hard to believe he'd missed three years of her life. He'd missed her first words, her first steps, and even her first day of preschool. Nothing could bring those moments back. Nothing. But he was determined to make up for them.

She went on for another five minutes before abruptly handing the phone back to her grandma. His mom laughed. "You should see her. She's staring out the window with the biggest smile on her face."

"She's excited," Jax said. "Call me if you need anything."

"I know how to handle a three-year-old. You were once that young, you know?" He could almost see her rolling her eyes through the phone.

"Sorry. I forget."

She snorted, but let it go. "Taylor told me you stopped by her house last night and helped put up the Christmas tree."

He heard the question behind her comment, but ignored it. "Taylor wanted me there, so she had Gabby call me."

His mom was silent.

Jax didn't know if that was because she didn't like his response or if she was waiting for him to say more. Either way, she was going to be disappointed. "I should get back to work."

There was an extended pause on the other end of the line before his mom responded. "All right. I'll let you go. I'll text you when we get checked in at the hotel."

"Love you, Mom."

"I love you, too, son. Take care of yourself."

He ended the call and sighed. His parents had no idea of his plans to talk to Gabby tonight. They'd get their hopes up if they knew and he didn't need the added pressure. He'd hurt Gabby by leaving, and at the very least he wanted to start rebuilding that trust with her. Explaining why he left was a step in the right direction. Even if he she would never let him into her heart again, they had to find a way to get past this tension. It wasn't good for Taylor.

Deep down, Jax hoped one day he'd be able to make it up to Gabby, to love her again the way she deserved. But for now he'd content himself with her being able to look him in the eye and not shrink away from him every time he came near. It was a lot to ask, he knew that, but he at least had to try. For Taylor's sake.

And for his own. He needed Gabby, and those three years without her in his life had only solidified that fact.

Chapter 4

Taylor's babysitter, Emily, sent Gabby a text letting her know Taylor's grandparents had picked her up. Gabby sent her a quick reply back, thanking her, and then went back to work on her novel. She'd called in sick to work figuring there was no way she'd be able to focus on her job knowing Jax was coming over that night to discuss custody arrangements—whatever that meant. So instead, after dropping her daughter off at preschool, Gabby drove back home and fired up her computer.

She'd been hoping working on her novel would distract her. Usually she was able to get lost in the words and shut out the outside world, but today she had no such luck. Her thoughts kept drifting to Jax. If she closed her eyes, she could almost feel his breath on her face, the feel of his body pressed against hers.

That wasn't to say she didn't get any writing done. She had. Without much effort, she'd written an entire chapter in less than two hours. That was a record. At least, for her.

Gabby scanned over the words on her screen and felt her internal temperature begin to rise. She pressed her legs together, desperate for friction as she continued to read. Everything she wanted to do with Jax—to have Jax do to her—was right there in black and white.

Her hand drifted down her belly to the button on her jeans. She pushed the button through the hole, releasing it, as her fingers dipped below her waistline.

The sound of her phone dinging brought her back to reality. As much as she'd have loved to let her mind continue down the path it was on, she couldn't ignore her phone. It could be about Taylor.

It wasn't. The text was from her mom letting her know she'd found Gabby's "Baby's First Christmas" ornament. Her mom had been more than a little distressed when she'd been putting up her tree and it wasn't in with the other ornaments.

Gabby typed out a swift reply.

I'm glad you found it. - Gabby

She was going to leave it at that, but then thought better of it.

Where was it? - Gabby

It was in the back of the closet behind some blankets. It must have fallen out of the box. - Caroline

:) - Gabby

The brief chat with her mother via text was enough to cool Gabby's libido. It was a good thing, too. When she looked at the clock, it was already after five. Jax would be there in less than an hour. She needed to have her head on straight when he got there.

Shutting down her computer, Gabby began tidying up. The house wasn't exactly a wreck, but it was amazing how much of a mess a three-year-old could create in a very short amount of time.

She was readjusting the pillows on the couch when her doorbell rang.

Without her permission, her pulse kicked up a notch. It always did whenever he was near. She wished she could turn it off, but so far she hadn't had much luck.

Gabby ran her hands along the front of her jeans before reaching for the doorknob.

He stood on her front porch, bundled up in a hat and gloves. It was only then she realized it was snowing.

She stepped back without a word, allowing him to enter.

"Thanks." He removed his hat. "It's actually coming down pretty good out there."

Gabby swallowed, trying to ignore how his hair was ruffled as if he'd just tumbled out of bed. "I thought we weren't supposed to get much."

He walked into the kitchen and placed the bags of food on the counter before removing his coat and gloves. "So did I." After draping his coat over one of the kitchen chairs, he went back to the food and began removing the containers from the bags. "I got your favorites."

She commanded her feet to move. "I'll get us some plates."

It felt like old times as they loaded their plates with Chinese food and sat at the table, eating. Only it wasn't like old times. They weren't a couple anymore. And he was there to talk about their daughter.

He took several bites of his food before he spoke. "Mom called me about an hour ago. They made it to the hotel and were heading out to get some dinner."

A lump formed in her throat. It had been hard enough getting used to her spending the weekend with Jax, but at least she was only a twenty-minute drive away. Knowing Taylor was in a completely different city without her was a new experience and Gabby wasn't sure she liked it.

Jax must have realized her discomfort. "She'll be okay."

"I know." Gabby shoveled another bite of food into her mouth. She waited until she'd swallowed before continuing. "It doesn't bother you at all, does it? Having her on the other side of the state?"

He wiped his mouth on a napkin. "I didn't say that."

"You sure don't act like it bothers you. You're sitting there all relaxed like you don't have a care in the world."

Jax sighed and abandoned his food to give her his full attention. She wasn't sure she liked that any better. "Gabby, I know this is hard. It is for me, too. My mom chastised me earlier and made it clear that Taylor will be fine. Besides, before long she's going to want to sleep over at a friend's house or go on school trips."

Gabby stood, suddenly not hungry anymore. "She'll be older then."

"Yes. But those people won't be family." He followed her into the kitchen, not letting her escape the way she desperately wanted to. "Mom will call if there are any problems, but she's going to be fine."

Placing her plate onto the counter with a little more force than she'd intended, Gabby spun on her heels to face him. "But what if she wakes up crying, wanting me? Or you? We won't be there."

Moisture filled her eyes and she had no way to stop it. She was missing her little girl, yes, but it wasn't only that. It was Jax being there as well. Having him in her home brought too many feelings to the surface.

"Gabby." He reached for her and she didn't stop him.

She held on to him, basking in the warmth and comfort he offered. "I don't know how my mother did it."

He rubbed her back in a soothing gesture as he continued to hold her. "Did what?"

"Let Grace and I go to camp. We'd be gone for an entire week."

Jax groaned. "I'm not ready to think about that yet. We've still got a few years."

His response made her feel a little better—like she wasn't the only one who was feeling anxious about their daughter growing up. "I know. But it feels like just yesterday that she was learning how to walk and say her first words."

He didn't say anything and it took her a minute to realize why.

Gabby started to pull back, but he stopped her. They stared into each other's eyes, their bodies still pressed together. A fact she was becoming highly aware of.

"I'm sorry," he whispered, his fingers teasing the hair around her ear.

Neither pulled away. A tiny voice in the back of her mind screamed for her to run away, to get as far away as she possibly could before she did something stupid again, but she couldn't get her limbs to work. Or maybe she didn't want to.

Her fingers brushed against the collar of his sweater and her gaze drifted to his mouth. It had been weeks since he'd kissed her, but she could still feel the pressure of his lips against hers.

He cupped the back of her head, tangling his fingers in her hair. "Gabby . . ."

She knew he felt it, too—the shift in the air around them. What had started out as comfort had changed into desire.

There were so many reasons why she should stop this, and the biggest reason was Taylor. They needed to keep things civil for her. She deserved that. She needed that.

But their daughter wasn't at the forefront of her mind at the moment. Gabby's nipples hardened at the memory of Jax's mouth on them . . . of his hands caressing her skin.

A moan escaped her lips and she felt his grip tighten. She opened her eyes and met his gaze. The same emotions she was feeling were reflected back at her.

Then she did something she would most likely regret. She grabbed the back of his head and tugged him toward her, sealing her lips to his in a searing kiss that left no doubt about the direction of her thoughts.

It took him a split second to catch up, but when he did, he didn't hold back. He crushed her body to him, not allowing any space between them. She lifted her leg, wrapping it around his waist, using the leverage to grind her pelvis against his erection.

Jax gasped, breaking their kiss. "Gabby." He was breathing hard as he stared into her eyes. "If we don't stop . . ."

She never broke eye contact. "I don't want to stop."

A moment later they were moving. He picked her up, wrapped her other leg around his waist, and carried her down the hall toward her bedroom.

***

Jax knew this would only complicate things, but at that moment he couldn't bring himself to care all that much. He wanted her and nothing else mattered except feeling her body surround him in every possible way.

On the way to her bedroom, he stubbed his toe on the doorjamb and had to stifle a groan. While it hurt, it didn't take long for the pain to take a back seat to the feel of Gabby against him. The weight of her breasts rubbing against his chest was extremely distracting.

As soon as he made it through her bedroom door, he headed for the bed. He was a little less than graceful as he lowered them onto the mattress, but she didn't seem to care any more than he did. With her newfound leverage, Gabby began rocking her hips against him, driving him mad.

He reached behind him, untangled her legs from around his waist, and immediately went to work on removing her jeans. It took him longer than it should have. Maybe it was because he was out of practice, or maybe because he was enjoying their kiss too much to divert his attention. He wanted his hands, his mouth, to be everywhere at once. It was always that way with her.

When he finally freed the button on her jeans, he lowered the zipper and she lifted her hips. He ripped his mouth away from hers long enough to remove her pants and throw them over his shoulder. Seconds later, he fell on top of her again, letting her feel his weight. He remembered she'd shared with him once how much she loved the weight of him pressing her into the mattress, and by her reaction that hadn't changed.

She snaked her hands between them and began unbuttoning his jeans. When her fingers brushed against his cock he sucked in a breath, trying to steady himself. He wasn't even sure she'd meant to do it, but his body didn't care.

As soon as he felt the zipper release, Jax pushed his jeans down his legs before kicking them the rest of the way off. She wasted no time circling her legs around him again and drawing their lower halves together. The feel of her against him, only two thin layers of fabric between them, was close to torture. He wanted to be inside her, but he also wanted to feel every inch of her first. It was a perplexing dilemma.

He felt her fingers dancing along the hem of his sweater and knew she wanted it off. Grabbing hold of the bottom of his sweater, he worked it up his torso and over his head, releasing her lips only long enough for the offending material to be removed.

Gabby flattened her palms over his chest and let her fingers explore. Everywhere she touched sent fire to his groin. He needed to touch her in the same way.

It took a little more maneuvering to remove her sweater and bra, but he managed with a little help from her. As if drawn to them like magnets, he cupped her breasts in both his hands, massaging them. He loved her breasts—not all that surprising since he was a guy, but it was so much more than that. He loved the way she arched her back as if begging him for emore. And he loved the little sounds she made at the back of her throat when he ran his thumbs over her nipples.

His cock was so hard in that moment that it was almost painful, but he wasn't ready to give in to his desire to be inside her quite yet. Releasing her lips, he lowered his mouth to cover her nipple. She threaded her fingers through his hair, holding him to her while he licked and sucked to his heart's content.

As he continued his assault on her breasts, her grinding against his cock increased. He released her nipple and rested his forehead against her chest as he tried to catch his breath. "You're going to kill me."

"Then get the rest of these clothes off us and fuck me already."

Jax laughed. He couldn't help himself. "Yes, ma'am."

Abandoning her breasts for the time being, he rocked back on his heels, took hold of her panties, and stripped them down her legs. Once she was completely naked, he wasted no time standing and removing his underwear as well. He fished a condom out of his jeans before climbing back onto the bed on top of her.

Gabby lay spread out before him, legs spread, waiting. He wanted to take the time to enjoy the view, but she wasn't having any part of it. She sat up, snatched the condom out of his hand, and ripped it open.

With the skill of someone who'd done it hundreds of times, she rolled the condom over his erection. He gritted his teeth trying not to explode solely from her touch.

She lay back and admired her work for a moment before hooking her leg around him again and urging him on top of her. He braced himself with one arm and used the other to guide himself to his goal.

Her soft warmth welcomed him as he eased into her pussy. Gabby opened her legs more, inviting him in and there was no way he was going to refuse. He thrust his hips, pushing his cock the rest of the way into her. It was a feeling he would never get used to and craved more than his next breath.

His lips found hers again as he began to move. Their flesh pushed and pulled as they moved against each other seeking pleasure and so much more. If nothing else, their bodies still knew the rhythm they'd perfected over the countless hours they'd spent exploring and loving each other.

She scraped her nails along his back and he gasped, almost losing his focus as the pain mixed with the pleasure coursing through him. He nibbled on her neck, knowing how much she loved it, and was rewarded with the feel of her digging her fingers into his shoulders. She was getting close and so was he.

Jax shifted his weight so he could get his hand between them and found her clit. She bucked against his hand. "Yes!"

"That's it, baby. Let go. Come for me."

He felt her inner muscles flex around him, driving him closer to his own climax.

Gabby's chest rose and fell more rapidly as she climbed higher and higher toward her goal. He held on to her just as tight, needing to have her close while he was given the chance. Jax knew that once they both came down from this high the tables would be turned and not in his favor. This wasn't how he'd wanted to start the night but had been powerless to stop it.

Several minutes passed as he increased the pressure on her clit in time with his thrusts before she tensed. A low whine passed her lips as she came apart in his arms. He captured her lips again with his own and let go. It didn't take long before he was following her over the edge.

Jax lay there on top of her, blood pumping through his veins, trying to catch his breath. He knew the moment the euphoria of her orgasm began to fade. Gabby removed her hands from his shoulders, holding them as if she didn't know quite where to put them. She cleared her throat. "I need to use the bathroom."

While he doubted that was actually the case, he rolled off her, freeing her to get up.

She scurried out of the bed and took off for the bathroom without looking back.

Sighing, Jax sat up on the bed and ran his fingers through his hair. He had no idea what he was going to do now. The point of tonight had been for them to talk—nothing more. He'd hoped it would be the first step to rebuilding trust. Somehow, he doubted what they'd just done would do anything to help facilitate that end goal.

He removed the condom and went to put it in the trash, then began gathering his clothes. By the time he'd finished dressing, Gabby still wasn't out of the bathroom.

Figuring he'd give her some time, he walked into the kitchen. The Chinese food he'd brought was still sitting out on the counter. He had no idea if she'd want to eat, but he was starving. Taking a plate, he loaded it up and popped it into the microwave.

He was sitting down at the table with his food when Gabby emerged from the hallway. Her eyes were red and a little puffy. She'd been crying.

All thought of being hungry left him. "Are you all right?"

She hugged herself as she met his gaze. "No."

Chapter 5

Gabby wanted to lock herself in the bathroom and not come out until he was gone, but she knew she couldn't do that. First of all, she doubted he'd leave until he saw her. Second, she wasn't a coward. So despite wanting to hide, she dried her tears and went to face him.

They stood on opposite sides of the room, staring at each other. He'd asked if she was all right and she'd been honest. She was anything but all right. He tied her up in knots, made her forget good sense, and generally made her crazy.

Jax took a step toward her and then seemed to think better of it. "Are you hungry? I warmed up some of the Chinese food."

She wasn't really, but it was that or asking him to leave, which she hadn't completely ruled out. "Sure."

He pushed the plate she knew he'd made for himself in her direction and motioned that she should have a seat while he got up to make himself a new plate. This was why it was so difficult to remind herself that she couldn't trust him. If it was an act, that would be different, but it wasn't. This was just Jax. He'd always put her first. Always.

Until the day he'd told her he was leaving town.

Pushing those thoughts aside, she picked up the fork he'd left behind and stabbed a piece of chicken. Her stomach didn't rebel, so she kept eating. After taking a couple more bites, she realized she was hungry after all.

The microwave dinged and Jax brought his new plate full of food to the table. They ate in silence for several minutes before he finally spoke. "I didn't mean for that to happen."

"I know." It would be so easy to blame him, but it wasn't his fault. Not entirely. Not at all, actually. After all, he had been the one to say it wasn't a good idea.

More awkward silence followed. It had been bad enough the first time it happened. She could write it off as a fluke, bad judgment. But for it to happen again? She couldn't dismiss it so easily. Was she doomed for the rest of her life to love a man who'd left her and their child?

Gabby didn't want to examine that too closely, so she did the only thing she could do. She deflected. "You said you wanted to come over tonight to talk about custody."

He released a breath loud enough for her to hear. "I want us to all be together on Christmas. I think Taylor needs that."

"How do you know what Taylor needs?" Gabby regretted her outburst the moment the words left her mouth. "I'm sorry. I shouldn't have—"

"Last weekend she had a nightmare."

"What?" Gabby asked, irritation mixing with concern for her daughter. "Why didn't you say something when you brought her home?"

"Because it was about me. Or not being able to find me, that is. Taylor said she'd dreamed that she searched everywhere and couldn't find me. She came to my room crying, so I let her sleep in my bed Saturday night."

Gabby didn't know what to say. She was upset and worried and wanted to hold her little girl and make sure she knew that no matter what, Gabby would always be there for her. "You should have told me."

"You're right. I should have. But it was over and I didn't want to upset you."

"So you wait to tell me until Taylor's two hours away and I can't do anything about it?" She pushed the plate away from her. Her food had lost all its flavor.

"Are you really mad because I didn't tell you our daughter had a nightmare or because we made love again?" His tone was matter of fact as he stared at her from across the table.

She didn't want to talk about what had happened tonight. Not now. Not ever. And definitely not with him. "I think you should go."

"We need to talk about this."

Pushing away from the table, Gabby stood and took her plate to the counter. She dug out some containers to put her uneaten food into, glad for something to do that put some space between them. "There's nothing to talk about."

He didn't answer right away, but when he did she felt him come up behind her. "I think there is."

Gabby closed her eyes, bracing herself for his touch and hating the fact that she craved it.

His hands wrapped around her forearms and he pressed his front to her back, the heat of him stirring her desire once again. This wasn't supposed to happen. She'd had three years to get over him and she thought she had. Until he'd waltzed back into their lives.

"I can't do this," she whispered.

"Can't do what?" His breath tickled the hairs at the back of her neck.

"This. Us."

He didn't back away. If anything, he leaned into her more, trapping her between his body and the counter. "I'm sorry I left you and Taylor, but at the time I thought it was the right thing."

Turning around, she looked him in the eyes. "The right thing? How could you possibly think leaving me and your child was the right thing?"

Something in his expression changed for a split second, and before she could get a read on what it was, he left her standing there and went to get his plate from where he'd left it on the table. He started gathering the food up, closing the containers, acting as if they hadn't been in the middle of a discussion. That was when it hit her that there might have been a reason why he'd left. Not because he was scared of being a father, which was what she'd always assumed, but a real, honest to goodness reason.

He brought his plate over and set it down beside hers. "Did you want to save this or just trash it?"

There was still a fair amount of food on his plate and she didn't want to be wasteful. Besides, it wasn't as if she hadn't swapped germs with him already.

Thinking about his mouth on hers had her lips tingling again. What was it about Jax? She'd been on two dates since he left, mainly just to get out of the house, and neither of them had come close to making her feel what he did simply by being in the same room with her.

She cleared her throat and concentrated on the task at hand. "Leave it. I can eat the leftovers tomorrow. It will save me from having to cook."

Once everything was in containers, she stuck them into the refrigerator. She'd been slowly putting things away, drawing it out as much as possible, to avoid their next awkward conversation. He'd come to talk about Christmas and he was right in that they needed to get on the same page.

Gabby thought he'd be sitting at the table waiting on her, but instead he was standing in the living room, looking out the window. As she drew closer, she realized he was frowning. "What is it?"

He motioned for her to look outside.

It took her a moment, but then she noticed it. Ice. The snow that had been falling when he'd arrived had changed to freezing rain and there was a thin coat of ice on everything. She knew what that meant. No matter how upset and hurt she was with him, there was no way she'd make him drive on a sheet of ice. Not when he didn't have to.

"I've got some extra blankets and a pillow in the closet. You can crash on the couch."

Jax glanced at her and then back outside. "I can probably make it to my apartment. It isn't that far."

She squared her shoulders, preparing for a fight. "No, you're not."

"It would be better if I left. We both know that."

"That's your answer to everything, isn't it?" Gabby huffed, turned on her heel, and marched down the hall. She opened the door to the closet and selected a fitted sheet, two blankets, a pillow, and a pillowcase.

When she made her way back into the living room with the armful of bedding, he was still standing at the window. She had just placed the items on the couch when he spoke. "I lied to you."

Gabby froze, her heart pounding. "What do you mean?"

He shoved his hands in his pockets and turned to face her. "I know when I left I made it sound as if I was scared of fatherhood, of all the unknowns it would bring, but that was a lie." He looked down at the floor and then back at her. "I left because I thought I was dying."

***

The look on Gabby's face had him wanting to take the words back. He shouldn't have said anything.

"Wh-what do you mean you were dying?" A million different emotions were playing across her face. He had no idea which one she'd settle on. For the moment, shock seemed to be winning out over the rest. Not that he could blame her. He'd felt the same way when he'd gotten the call.

"Do you remember the morning about a week before I left when I ran to the store to get diapers and baby wipes?"

She nodded.

"On the way home, I got a call from my doctor. You remember I'd been having those headaches."

Gabby sucked in a loud breath and he knew she remembered. He used to sit with his head in her lap, her massaging his temples when they got really bad.

"I went in to see a specialist, hoping they could find out why I was getting them." He knew it was better to get it all out. Better to rip off the Band-Aid in one go. "They found a mass pressing against my spine near the base of my skull."

All color left Gabby's face, and she reached for the arm of the couch and sat down. It took her a minute to get her bearings. "Cancer?"

"Luckily, no. But I didn't know that at the time. I didn't know much of anything except that the doctor said it needed to be removed or the headaches would continue to get worse." Jax took a deep breath. "He said it was high risk, given where the mass was located. If something went wrong with the surgery, I might not be able to walk, talk, take care of myself . . . and that was assuming it wasn't cancer."

She wasn't looking at him. In fact, he wasn't sure she was looking at much of anything.

He crossed the room and took a seat next to her on the couch. After several minutes passed and she didn't say anything, he touched her arm.

Her reaction was swift and immediate. She jerked her arm away from him and stood, putting several feet between them. When she faced him, her eyes were blazing with anger. "Don't you dare touch me."

"I'm sorry. I was just worried about you. You were so quiet—"

"You were worried about me? Worried? You stopped having a right to be worried about me when you walked out that door three years ago."

He held his hands in front of him, pleading with her to understand. "I didn't do it to hurt you. It was the last thing I wanted. But I didn't want to be a burden to you and Taylor. She was so small and she needed you. I couldn't take you away from her."

Gabby got a hard look on her face. She pressed her lips together in a thin line and narrowed her eyes. "So instead you took yourself away from both of us."

Before he could decide how to respond to that, she marched in the direction of her bedroom. He didn't follow her.

Running a frustrated hand over his head, he contemplated driving home again, but decided against it. Not only was it dangerous, but he needed to fix things with Gabby. While he had little hope they would ever have the type of relationship they'd had before, they did need to find a way to interact for Taylor's sake.

Jax took the bedding Gabby had brought out for him and began making up the couch. It crossed his mind that her bed would be a lot more comfortable, but quickly quashed that train of thought. If he walked into her bedroom right then he'd probably get something chucked at his head.

He kicked off his shoes, stripped down to his boxers, and slipped under the blanket. Staring up at the ceiling, he listened to the sounds of the house. Every now and then he thought he heard Gabby moving around in her bedroom, and he ached to go to her.

He closed his eyes and groaned in frustration. This was going to be a long night.

The sound of Gabby's phone ringing had him sitting up. He heard her talking, but he couldn't make out what she was saying. Given the time, it was most likely Taylor.

His suspicions were confirmed when, not long after he heard her stop talking, his cell rang. "Hey."

"Have you talked to Gabby lately?" his mother asked, not bothering with pleasantries.

"Yeah. We talked earlier. Why?" There was no way he was going to tell his mom that he was currently on Gabby's couch.

"I hung up with her a minute ago and . . . I don't know. She didn't sound like herself. Did you notice anything when you talked to her?"

He hated lying to his mother, but in this case he was going to make an exception. Or, at least, not be completely truthful. "Maybe you caught her in the middle of something."

"I don't think that was it. Maybe you should call her. It's still early."

"Mom, Gabby and I aren't a couple anymore. I'm sure she wouldn't appreciate me sticking my nose into her business."

"Yes, but—"

"Mom." He waited for a moment to make sure she was listening. "I know you mean well, but Gabby and I have to navigate through things in our own way. You need to respect that."

His mom sighed. "I just want to see you both happy again like you were when you were together. That day in the hospital after Taylor was born was the happiest I'd ever seen either of you."

Jax didn't say anything because there was nothing to say. He recalled the moment she was referring to. His heart had been full of love for Gabby, Taylor, and their future together as a family. The engagement ring he'd bought the week before was burning a hole in his pocket, but he wanted to wait until he was able to take her out for a nice dinner and propose the right way. The phone call from his doctor had come before he'd gotten the chance.

Needing to change the subject, he asked how things were going in Kansas City.

"She seems to like it so far. The weather put a wrench in our dinner plans, so we just ordered pizza and stayed in the hotel. She's having fun channel surfing with Grandpa." He heard her chuckle, and then her voice sounded farther away. "Taylor, did you want to say good night to Daddy?"

A few seconds later, his daughter's voice filled his ears. "Hi, Daddy."

"Hi, Pumpkin. Are you having fun with Grandma and Grandpa?"

He could hear the phone being moved and imagined she was probably nodding her head. "We's order pizza 'cause it was rainin' and Gran'ma didn't want to get her hair wet."

Jax bit the inside of his lip to keep from laughing. "Well, I'm glad you didn't get wet."

Their conversation went on for a few more minutes with Taylor telling him about the big trucks she saw on the way there. He loved hearing the way she saw the world.

By the time he said good night and placed his cell on the table nearby, he had almost forgotten about what had happened with Gabby. Almost.

There were no longer sounds coming from her room and he wondered if she was asleep or if she was lying there thinking about the fact that he'd been in her bed only a couple of hours ago. His mind immediately went to how it felt to have her under him again. No matter how much he tried to convince himself this thing between them was over, the pull he felt toward her wouldn't let up, and it seemed to be the same for her.

Flopping onto his back, he tried to push away the memories and the hope that came with them. He wanted her. He always had. Leaving hadn't changed that. And coming back sure as hell hadn't either.

He had no idea how long he lay there, his mind going a million miles a minute, before he threw off the blanket and padded down the hall to her bedroom. The door was closed and the lights were off, but he could have sworn he heard the muffled sound of crying.

"Gabby? Are you okay?" he asked.

"I'm fine. Go to sleep." Her voice shook slightly and he knew he'd been right. His heart broke and all he wanted to do was comfort her.

Placing his palm flat on the door, he leaned his forehead against it and closed his eyes. She wasn't going to accept his comfort. Not now.

He lifted his head, looking at the door in front of him—the door that separated them. If only that was the thing keeping them apart. A physical barrier could be removed.

Jax released a heavy breath, removed his hand, and whispered, "Good night, Gabby," before heading back to his makeshift bed on the couch.

Chapter 6

Gabby held her breath until she heard Jax walk away. A fresh tear rolled down her cheek and she brushed it away with the back of her hand. She was so mad at him. Furious. Enraged. She didn't think there were enough words in the English dictionary to describe how she was feeling. That's how upset she was.

Before she'd thought it was fear of being a father that had sent him running. She'd said as much at the time and he hadn't corrected her. That had been bad enough, although on some level she could understand it. She'd been scared herself as a first-time mom, but she figured they'd get through it. Together.

So many thoughts were flooding her mind, including the fact that he could have gone off and died and she might never have known. That ticked her off more than anything. How could he have done that? Didn't at least his daughter deserve to know if he'd died?

A part of her wanted to charge out there and give him a piece of her mind. The more rational part, however, knew that wouldn't solve anything.

She sat up and turned on the light beside her bed. The hall was quiet, so she figured he'd gone to sleep. It had been a while since he'd stood outside her door. According to the clock on her nightstand, it had been over an hour.

Trying to make as little noise as possible in case he was still up, Gabby made her way across the hall and into the bathroom. She waited until after she'd closed the door before turning on the light.

It took a few seconds for her eyes to adjust, and then she went to the sink to wash her face. She was hoping that maybe that would help calm her down enough so she could go to sleep. Normally, she'd make herself some chamomile tea, but that would mean going to the kitchen and possibly waking Jax. She was just going to have to get by without it.

The mirror above the sink showcased the damage an hour-long crying jag could do to one's complexion. Gabby's eyes were red and swollen and her entire face was blotchy. All she needed were a few zits to go with it to round off the look.

She turned on the water, leaving it a little on the cold side, and splashed some onto her face. It helped. Some. But it didn't work miracles.

After blotting her face dry and putting on some moisturizer, hoping it would help balance out the blotches, she reached for the doorknob and turned off the light. She opened the door and stepped out into the hall. Right into Jax.

She wobbled slightly and he grabbed hold of her forearms to steady her. Gabby hated to admit it, but even after everything she'd learned tonight her body still reacted to his touch. It didn't help that he was standing there in nothing but his boxers.

As soon as the direction of her thoughts registered, she pulled away, almost falling flat on her butt. Luckily, she backed into the doorframe and she used it to keep herself upright. "What are you doing up?"

He acted as if he wanted to reach for her again, but lucky for her, he kept his hands to himself. "I was going to ask you the same question. I heard you up moving around and wanted to make sure you were okay."

"I told you earlier I was fine." It was so much easier lying when he wasn't standing right there in front of her.

"You've been crying."

She didn't see a point in trying to deny it. The proof was right in front of him. "Yes."

Jax raised his hand as if he was going to cup her face, but halfway there he closed it into a fist and lowered it back down to his side. "I hate that I hurt you. It's not what I wanted. I wanted . . ."

Gabby waited, but he didn't go on. "I need to get back to bed."

When she went to push past him, he stopped her, his body blocking her path. Her heart rate sped up as he moved in closer. If any other man did this to her, she would be filled with fear. With Jax, her body was screaming *"take me"* even while her mind was trying to get her legs to run as quickly as possible. Her body was winning.

This time he did reach up and cup the side of her face, tilting her head so she would meet his gaze. "I didn't want you to suffer with me and I knew you would. I wanted to spare you from the pain of watching me die. I couldn't do that to you."

Her nipples, hard and ready with him this close, rubbed against his naked chest, sending an electric shock directly to her sex. She sucked in a breath and closed her eyes, trying to focus.

"I'm sorry, Gabby. You can't know how sorry I am." He leaned in, his lips beckoning her. It would be so easy to forget—lose herself in him again.

As tempting as it was, she couldn't do it. "So you made the decision for me."

That seemed to bring him up short. He looked down at her, confused.

With a little room to breathe, Gabby was able to think more clearly. "You didn't trust me to make the decision for myself, so you made it for me."

"That's not—"

"That's exactly what you did." Gabby stepped out of his arms, feeling her anger return. She concentrated on that and not his half-naked body. "You didn't trust me to decide for myself, to decide what was best for me."

He seemed stunned by her outburst, but she kept going.

"You had no right to decide for me, Jax. None. It was my decision and you took it away from me."

Before he could respond, Gabby ducked under his arm and made a beeline for her bedroom. She slammed the door shut and turned the lock, something she rarely ever did, and let her back slide along the wood as she lowered herself to the floor.

Several minutes passed with no sound coming from the hallway. It was like a replay of earlier that night, except she wasn't crying this time. Of course, as soon as she heard his footsteps retreating down the hall, her anger began to dissipate, leaving her feeling raw and exposed.

She'd heard the saying 'rip your heart out' over the years, and she'd thought she understood it after Jax left the first time, but what she was feeling now was much worse. He'd chosen for her, not trusting that she would do what was right for her and her baby. It was as if the wounds from him leaving three years ago, wounds she'd worked desperately to heal, had been ripped open again and had salt poured into them.

Forcing herself up, she went to her desk and turned on her computer. There was no way she was going to be able to sleep, so she might as well do something productive. It was a good thing she was in the middle of writing a shootout between the hero and the bad guys. She needed to get out some of her frustration, and what better way than to kill some fictional characters? It was a better option than breaking something over the head of a certain man who was currently sleeping on her couch, which sounded pretty good at the moment.

Gabby closed her eyes, took a deep breath, and let her fingers dance over the keys. She poured all her anger out, letting it consume her hero as he closed in on one of the bad guys. By the time she finished the scene, her hero was covered in blood with four dead bodies lying at his feet, but Gabby had to admit she felt a little better.

As she sat there staring at the words she'd written, she began to feel the lateness of the hour. She knew she needed to at least try and get a few hours' sleep.

After saving her work, she powered down her computer and stood, stretching her stiff muscles. She'd been sitting in the same position for hours.

Gabby could barely keep her eyes open as she crossed the room to her bed.

The mattress dipped when she crawled under the covers. She rested her head on her pillow, letting its softness soothe her even more. Within seconds, she was asleep.

***

It was a long night. Jax ended up spending most of it staring at the Christmas tree. The lights weren't on, but it was better than staring at the ceiling.

He kept replaying what Gabby had said over and over in his mind. Was she right? Had he not trusted her? It hadn't played out that way in his head at the time, but he did recall his mom saying something along those lines.

Eventually, the first rays of the sun began peeking through the curtains and he decided sleep wasn't going to come for him. He slipped on his jeans, folded the sheet and blanket Gabby had given him the night before, and placed them on the end of the couch with his pillow. Then he went to the kitchen to see what he could dig up for breakfast.

Gabby's refrigerator contained everything he needed to make a decent breakfast. He pulled out the eggs, milk, ham, cheese, and found some potatoes and onions in her pantry. Considering how early it was, Jax didn't figure Gabby would be up for a while but that didn't mean he couldn't fix something for both of them. Besides, it might help him get back in her good graces again. That was probably wishful thinking on his part, but it couldn't hurt.

Jax turned the oven on to preheat and took his time cutting the ham, potatoes, and onions before mixing them together with the eggs, milk, and cheese. By the time he had everything combined, the oven was ready. He poured everything into a glass baking dish, covered it with tinfoil, and popped it in to cook.

Once that was done, he was left wondering how he should pass the time. He wanted to check on Gabby, but something told him that wasn't such a good idea. She'd been pissed at him last night. The last thing he wanted was to make it worse.

A brief look outside told him that things hadn't improved much during the night. Icicles hung from the tree branches and car mirrors. A glance at the roads confirmed that the snow plows hadn't been through and he doubted they'd see them anytime soon. If the rest of the city was like this, the salt crews would have their hands full making sure the main roads were clear.

Jax picked up his phone from where he'd left it on the coffee table and checked his email. He'd gotten eight new messages in the last twelve hours, five of them from clients. If he'd known he was going to be stuck here for any length of time, he would have brought his laptop.

Two hours later, his belly full of the breakfast casserole he'd made, he sat on the couch, flipping through channels on the television, trying to find something decent to watch that wasn't cartoons. That was where Gabby found him. Or, at least, that's where he was when she strolled out of her bedroom. She completely ignored him and walked into the kitchen.

He debated for a split second whether or not to give her some space but decided against it. Taking his time, he made his way into the kitchen and rested his elbows on the island. "I made breakfast casserole."

She opened the dishwasher and began putting dishes away. Once she'd finished with that, she went to the refrigerator, took out the orange juice, and poured herself a glass.

"Are you not talking to me this morning?" he asked.

"There's nothing to say."

Gabby didn't even bother to look at him. She did, however, lift up the foil on the casserole. He wondered for a moment if she was going to pass on it, but she got a plate out of the cabinet and scooped out a healthy portion for herself.

After heating her food up in the microwave, she brought her plate to the table and sat down, bypassing Jax.

He went to take the seat across from her. While he wanted to continue their conversation from last night, he thought he'd start out with something a little safer. "The roads are still covered with ice. I'm honestly surprised we didn't lose power."

She glanced up at him, and then went back to her food.

"It looks like I'm going to be stuck here for a little while longer."

Nothing.

"Are you planning to ignore me all day?"

Gabby finished swallowing and took a drink of her orange juice before she spoke. "I haven't decided yet."

"I think we need to talk."

Again, she remained silent.

He waited until her plate was empty. "I was wrong."

That seemed to get her attention. Or at least he thought it did until she stood and took her plate to the sink without saying a word.

Jax pushed away from the table and followed her into the kitchen. "I thought about what you said and you were right. I should have talked to you . . . told you what the doctor said. It was wrong of me to take that choice away from you."

She stilled, her gaze never leaving her hands.

It was now or never. Jax knew he needed to put it all out there because if he didn't, he might never get another chance. "I was scared. Terrified. When I found out, I didn't know what to do. The doctor wanted to see me again to discuss my options. I almost didn't go. I might not have if not for my dad."

"You told your dad, but not me." It was the first sign she was actually listening to him.

"I don't know why, but yes. As soon as I got the call I drove to his work and waited for him."

Gabby pressed her lips together and gripped the sink in front of her. He knew he'd hurt her again.

"We sat in the parking lot until sunset and he convinced me to keep the appointment." Jax shook his head and took a step closer, longing to reach out for her but knowing he shouldn't. "The doctor said my best chance was to go to a hospital in Chicago. They were doing some cutting-edge stuff with lasers and he said it was my best chance at getting the mass removed without causing permanent damage."

He saw her blink and hoped she wasn't going to start crying. There was no way he'd be able to stop himself from trying to comfort her if he saw tears.

"It took me three days to decide to do as the doctor suggested and go to Chicago." He didn't hold anything back. "I told you I had to go see a client."

"I don't want to hear any more." She spun on her heels and practically ran to her bedroom.

Jax hightailed it right after her. He'd run away three years ago and look where it had gotten them.

The door to her room began closing in his face and he thrust his hand out to stop it.

"Leave me alone, Jax. I don't want to talk," she yelled through the semi-closed door.

"That's too bad because I'm not going anywhere. We need to talk about this."

"No, we don't. It doesn't matter anymore. You left. What more is there to say?" He could have sworn he heard some of the same shakiness in her voice from the night before, and suddenly her running away made sense. She didn't want him to see her cry again.

"I'm coming in." It was all the notice he gave before pushing the door open and walking inside.

Gabby stood near the center of the room, her face flushed and her eyes full of moisture. "Why are you doing this?"

"Because I need to tell you. It's been hanging between us and we can't keep dancing around it." It was killing him to keep his hands to himself, but he managed it somehow. "Taylor deserves better than two parents who avoid each other whenever possible."

"I don't—"

"Yes. You do," he said in the gentlest tone possible.

Sitting down on the edge of her bed, she crossed her arms and fixed him with a hard stare. "Fine. Let's talk. Did you even think about telling me the truth back then?"

"Yes."

"So why didn't you?"

He saw the fire in her eyes again and knew he needed to tread lightly. "I didn't want to scare you if it was nothing, so I wanted to wait and see what the other doctor in Chicago said. I was hoping the specialist I'd seen here in St. Louis was wrong."

She waited.

"While I was waiting to see the new doctor, I couldn't help but look around. Almost everyone there was with someone—a husband, a wife, a parent. They varied in age to not much older than me to my parents' age. But the one thing they had in common was how worn out they looked. They all looked exhausted. I knew if the doctor didn't have good news for me that this would be my fate, too. Our fate."

Unable to handle being so far away from her any longer, Jax took a seat beside her on the bed. She stiffened. He didn't know if she was bracing herself for whatever came next, or if she feared what would happen if he touched her. Especially considering where they were.

"The doctor laid it all out for me. Best case scenario would more than likely include months of physical therapy." He sighed. "I couldn't do that to you. Or Taylor. So I chose to leave you both, hoping that if I made it I could come back to you."

Chapter 7

Gabby was trying her best to hold on to her temper. "And what if things didn't go well? Huh? You could have died and we never would have known."

"Yes, you would have. And you would have been taken care of. I'd made sure of that. Even before I went to Chicago, I updated my will to make you and Taylor my sole beneficiaries. The life insurance would have—"

She stood abruptly. "Do you think I care about that? That somehow money would have made it better if we had lost you?" Tears were streaming down her face again and there was nothing she could do to stop them.

"I didn't mean—"

"Of course you didn't. You didn't mean anything."

Jax eased himself into a standing position, almost as if he were afraid if he moved too fast he would spook her. "I'm sorry. I didn't mean to hurt you. That was the opposite of what I wanted. But I thought a little hurt now would save you from a bigger hurt later. I see now that I was wrong." Stepping forward, he placed his hands on her forearms and waited until she looked at him. "If I could go back and do it over, I would do things differently, but I can't. All I can do is say I'm sorry and try to make it up to you if I can."

"How?" She sniffed, hating that she was such an emotional mess. "How are you going to make it up to us?"

"I want to be a good dad to Taylor. To be there for her when she needs me. To see her grow up, and even to help chase the boys away when she's old enough to start dating."

Gabby couldn't help but chuckle at that.

He slid his hands up her arms and cupped her face between his palms. "I promise I won't take off again."

"I don't know if I can trust you." She whispered the words because that was all she could manage at the moment. The pull she always felt toward him was there, even though seconds ago she was ready to throttle him.

A small step forward closed the gap between them until their chests were touching. "Give me time. I'll prove it to you."

She closed her eyes, trying to steady herself—an almost impossible task when he was standing so close to her. "I don't know . . ."

"Please, Gabby. Give me one more chance. I promise you won't regret it."

His mouth was a breath away from hers. It would be so easy to give in—to let her hormones take control again. But she'd done that before. Twice. And it had gotten them nowhere.

Before she could talk herself out of it, Gabby pulled away.

He didn't reach for her again, letting his arms fall to his sides.

She took a deep breath, trying to clear her head. Every time he was near her entire body went into hyperdrive. "I need some time to think."

Jax looked disappointed but nodded anyway. "I understand."

They stood there for several minutes, the air between them becoming charged again. She knew they needed to get out of her bedroom. "Have you checked the weather this morning?"

"Not much change from last night. They're asking people to stay off the streets so the plows can salt the roads."

Gabby moved to her dresser. "I'm going to shower and then see if I can get some writing done."

"I'll try to stay out of your way." With that, he turned and walked out of the room, leaving her alone.

Grabbing a clean pair of underwear, bra, and a change of clothes, Gabby headed for the bathroom. Once the door was closed behind her, she felt as if she could breathe again. Or at least, better. Knowing they were both stuck there for the time being wasn't helping. She didn't like feeling trapped in general, but with all the emotions flooding through her she felt as if she'd been thrown into the deep end of a pool without knowing how to swim to the other side.

Warm steam filled the room as she removed her pajamas and threw them into the hamper that was almost overflowing. She'd need to do laundry today. It would give her something to do to take her mind off Jax. As much as she wanted to write, she wasn't sure she would be able to focus. She'd written the big fight scene the night before and all that was left was the final reunion of the two main characters. Given the intensity of the story's climax, and its tone, it needed to be both sweet and sexy and Gabby wasn't feeling either of those at the moment.

Okay, she was feeling somewhat sexy. It was impossible not to when Jax looked at her the way he did—like he wanted to rip her clothes off right then and there.

Gabby groaned when she realized the direction her thoughts were taking. It was always like this. All she had to do was think about him and she began remembering all the things he could do to her body.

Grabbing her shower gel, Gabby added a large dollop to her loofah. She kneaded the gel into the fibers with a little water until it was covered in suds and ran it over her skin. Even though her loofah felt nothing like Jax's hands, the sensation lit up the nerve endings in her arms, stomach, and breasts. She was a hot ball of arousal by the time she rinsed herself off.

There was only a moment's hesitation before she reached for the removable showerhead. She'd invested in one not long after Jax left. With a baby in the house, the shower was one of the few times she had to herself and she'd made the most of it.

She turned the dial on the showerhead from the gentle spray she used to wash to something with a little more pressure behind it. Then she rested her back against the side of the shower and spread her legs. The moment the water hit her already sensitive clit, she had to bite her lip to keep from moaning.

Closing her eyes, she let her mind go where it wanted. She could feel his hands ghosting over her body, coaxing her closer and closer to orgasm.

Her body heated at memories of him between her legs, running his tongue over her sex, circling her clit. It had been so long since she'd felt his mouth on her like that.

Gabby gasped as her grip on the showerhead slipped a little and the water hit a new spot. She blindly searched for something to hold on to as she climbed higher toward her goal. *Oh.*

Every muscle in her body clenched and she yelled out as she reached her climax. All of the want and need she'd been feeling finally found release. She lowered the showerhead and sagged against the wall as her breathing slowly returned to normal.

Once her head began to clear, Gabby knew she was in trouble. As much as she feared being hurt again, she wasn't sure if she could resist Jax. Not for long anyway. Every cell in her being responded to him.

She finished washing up and took her time getting dressed. Giving in would be so easy. But was that what was best for her and Taylor? He said he wouldn't leave again, but could she trust that? Would she ever be able to trust *him*?

The problem was she didn't know the answer to any of those questions. She wanted him, yes. That didn't mean, however, that opening her heart to him was a good idea.

But what was the alternative? Continue how they'd been? He was right about the way they'd been tiptoeing around each other. At the moment Taylor was too young to pick up on it, but sooner or later she'd be able to figure out something wasn't right between her parents. What then?

She ran a brush through her hair as she blew it dry with the hair dryer. It was a mindless task, which was good. She needed all her mental energy to figure out what she was going to do about Jax.

The more she thought about it, the more she realized there was only one thing she could do. She was going to have to give him the chance he'd asked for. It scared her more than anything had in her life except giving birth to her daughter. That had turned out to be one of the best things to ever happen to her. She could only hope this thing with Jax turned out the same.

Her hair mostly dry, she put everything away and opened the door. She halted when she saw Jax a few feet away, leaning against the opposite wall.

Gabby opened her mouth to ask him what he was doing standing there when she got a look at his eyes. His stance might have been casual, but his eyes told a different story. She lowered her gaze to his crotch and sure enough she could see the bulge of his erection.

Before she could find her words, he spoke, his voice husky and full of lust. "I heard you scream and thought you needed help."

Her eyes went wide and her heart rate skyrocketed. She knew she was in trouble. Big, big trouble.

***

Jax watched the range of emotions fly across Gabby's face. She sucked in a lungful of air, causing her breasts to rise and fall. The sweater she was wearing did little to lessen the impact to his libido. He knew what was underneath the thick fabric.

Her lips parted and her tongue darted out to run along her bottom lip before disappearing back inside her mouth. He swallowed, trying to hold on to his resolve to give her the space she'd asked for. It wasn't easy, but he held his ground.

That was until she launched herself at him. She took hold of his face, pulling it down until her lips covered his. It took him a moment to catch up to the change, but when he did he held nothing back. He wrapped his arms around her, crushing her against him as he devoured her mouth.

Gabby pressed against him, pushing his weight into the wall. There was an almost frantic feeling to her kiss . . . a desperation. As much as he loved her enthusiasm, he didn't want her to end up regretting it like she had last night.

He ripped his mouth free for a second. "Gabby."

She kissed him again, dipping her tongue into his mouth. It would be so easy to forget his worries and go with it, but he didn't just want to lose himself in her body. She was more important to him than a moment of pleasure.

"I don't," he said between kisses. "Want. You. To. Regret."

Gabby stopped and met his gaze. He could see the hunger in her eyes, the want. But that had never been the problem. For either of them. He'd wanted her from the first moment he saw her and it had been the same for her. He doubted that would ever change. "I won't regret it."

"You said that last time and—"

She placed two fingers over his lips. "I promise I won't go hide in the bathroom after." Her gaze went to his lips. "I promise we'll talk. Later." She looked up at him again. "Right now I need you. There is only so much a showerhead can do."

His cock pulsed at the image she'd presented, the sound of her scream still fresh in his mind. He cupped her ass with the palm of his left hand and her breast with the other.

Gabby arched her back, thrusting her breast farther into his hand.

He couldn't resist such a temptation. Lowering his mouth, he moaned as their lips connected once more. She stood on her tiptoes and lifted her leg to wrap around his hip, seeking the friction she desired.

They kissed until he couldn't stand it anymore. He needed to touch her bare skin, to feel her warmth without her clothes blocking his access.

"What do you want?" he asked.

Never one to shy away from expressing her feelings, Gabby answered him. "I want you to use your mouth to make me come." Then she said something that was sure to make what little room he had in his jeans disappear. "That's what I was thinking about in the shower. You between my legs. The way your tongue—"

She yelped as he kissed her hard, cutting her off, and then picked her up and carried her into her bedroom. He laid her down on the bed and immediately reached for the button on her pants.

Gabby giggled as he lowered her zipper and worked the jeans down her legs. He dropped them on the floor and went to work on ridding her of the panties. It was then she seemed to decide to help speed up the process. She reached for the hem of her sweater and shimmied it up her torso and over her head.

Spreading her legs, Jax settled himself between them and let her scent fill his lungs. He met her gaze and held it as he ran his tongue along her pussy. "You're so beautiful like this. All spread out for me." He took another long lick, savoring her flavor.

As he continued to feast on her, she closed her eyes and tilted her head back. Gabby arched her back and placed her hand on top of his head, encouraging him. She didn't have to worry. He had no desire to stop.

The last time he'd been in that position was shortly before she'd given birth to Taylor. Her contractions had started, but they weren't close enough together to warrant going to the hospital yet. He remembered feeling helpless and needing to do something to help her. It had started out with him massaging her back and belly. Then she'd mentioned reading something about sex helping move labor along. He'd been hesitant, but as time passed and her contractions continued, he thought of a compromise that ended up being exactly what they'd both needed.

"Please." She dug her fingernails into his scalp, urging him on.

"Are you getting close, baby?"

"Uh-huh." Jax thought he saw her nod, but he couldn't be sure. He was too focused on what he was doing.

A few more circles around her clit and she was teetering on the edge. Her breathing was labored and he could feel a slight tremor in her legs.

"That's it. Let go. Come for me, Gabby. I want to hear you. Don't hold back." He flattened his tongue over her clit, took a long lick, and then sucked it into his mouth.

She inhaled a lungful of air and pushed his head toward her body, begging him not to let up on his assault.

Jax couldn't help but smile. He thrust two fingers inside her, putting pressure right where she liked it. The low moan coming from her throat let him know he'd hit the correct spot.

"Jax?"

He sucked harder. Added a little more pressure.

"Jax!"

The walls of her pussy pulsed around his fingers as they coated him with moisture. He eased up on her clit, softly bringing her down from her high.

Jax removed his fingers and placed them into his mouth. She tasted amazing and she looked amazing lying there, her skin flushed a lovely pink color as she worked to slow her breathing.

Her gaze followed his movements, watching him lick the evidence of her orgasm. "Watching you do that is such a turn-on."

He chuckled and eased himself on top of her, bringing his face level with hers. "You like that, do you?"

She circled her arms around his neck, pulling his mouth down for a kiss. "Yes."

Since meeting Gabby, he'd learned that she didn't hold back once she decided to go after something. It didn't matter if it was in life or in the bedroom.

She probed his mouth, exploring and tasting herself on his tongue. He deepened the kiss, encouraging her to continue her search.

"You're wearing too many clothes," she murmured against his lips. Snaking her hands between them, she began pulling at the hem of his sweater.

Jax sat up and removed the offending piece of material. "So are you."

"I'm naked except for my bra."

"Exactly."

Gabby rolled her eyes but turned to one side so he could unhook her bra. She tossed it aside, leaving her without a stitch of clothing. "Satisfied?"

A wicked look crossed his face. "Not yet."

It took some maneuvering, but he kicked his shoes, socks, and pants off before returning to hover over her. "Please tell me you have condoms somewhere. I used the only one I had last night."

She turned her head to look at her nightstand and lifted her chin. "Top drawer."

When he opened the drawer, he found a small box of condoms. He breathed a sigh of relief when he saw they'd never been opened.

Gabby helped him push his boxers down his legs and out of the way. Before he was able to get the condom out of the wrapper, she took hold of his cock and began moving her hand from base to tip. He grabbed the back of her neck and kissed her hard, pumping his hips into her hand.

The head of his erection bumped her opening and Jax knew he needed to get the condom on before they both ended up losing their heads. As much as he would love to have another child someday, he doubted Gabby was ready for that. He wasn't even sure they were a couple at this point and he didn't want to add to their issues. They had enough obstacles to overcome as it was.

He nudged her hand away and rolled the condom over his erection. Once it was in place, he wasted no time. He lined himself up with her entrance and let his cock sink into her warmth.

"Kiss me," Gabby demanded as his cock was swallowed up by her pussy.

Thrusting his hips forward, he lowered himself down, covering her body with his as he brought their lips together. They moved, connected like that. It was so much more than finding pleasure in each other. There had always been so much more with Gabby.

His feelings for her overwhelmed him until he couldn't contain them anymore. "I love you. I always have. I never stopped."

She cupped the side of his face, staring into his eyes. "I love you, too. I never stopped."

There was a charge in the air around them that went beyond the physical and neither one seemed to be able to look away. They continued to move the lower halves of their bodies, their rhythm increasing as the sensations built within them.

When he could tell she was getting close, he lowered his right hand and placed it on her hip. He found her clit with his thumb and began to massage it in time with their thrusts.

A few minutes later she was falling apart in his arms, and he followed her soon after.

Chapter 8

Jax held his breath as he eased off Gabby, removed the condom, and threw it in the small trash can she kept near her bed. Even though she'd said she wouldn't regret it afterward, he had his doubts. But instead of racing off to the bathroom like she had the night before, Gabby rolled over to face him.

"You okay?" he asked when she didn't say anything.

"Thinking."

He flipped to his side so he could see better. "About?"

"Us."

The one word back and forth wasn't really getting them anywhere, so he decided to take a different tack. "Are you having second thoughts about—"

"No." She averted her eyes, looking off into the distance. "I meant what I said before."

Not liking the separation, he reached for her hand and laced their fingers together.

She returned her gaze to him. "I'm still hurt you didn't talk to me before you left. That you didn't tell me—"

"I know. I can't tell you how sor—"

"Let me finish."

"Sorry." Jax shut up and let her talk.

"As much as I might hate to admit it, this thing between us never went away. And I'm not sure it ever will. I will probably love you until the day I die. Maybe longer than that." She sighed. "I know that might sound pathetic to some, given the circumstances, but there it is. I'm tired of fighting it."

"So does that mean you want to give us another shot?"

Gabby was quiet for a long moment. "Yes."

He leaned in to kiss her, but she pulled back. The hope that had been blooming in his chest was replaced with anxiety.

"No more secrets."

"I promise."

He went in again for that kiss, but once more she thwarted him. "I mean it."

"I know." He cupped the back of her head with his free hand. "I promise to be a good boy from now on."

She giggled and playfully pushed at his chest as his mouth descended upon hers.

By the time their lips separated, they'd inched their way closer to each other until their bodies were intertwined once more. One of his arms was cradling the back of her head while he had the other hand holding on to one of her ass cheeks. Maybe it wasn't the best position to have this type of conversation, but he had no desire to release her. Not after all this time.

"I missed you," she whispered. "I missed this."

"I won't leave you again."

"You better not. I might have to take drastic measures."

He ran his hand up her back and down again. "Understood."

They lay there touching for several minutes before she spoke again. "I don't think we should tell Taylor yet. I don't want to get her hopes up."

Her words hit him like a kick in the gut. "You don't think it will work between us?"

"You hurt me, Jax." Her words did nothing to help the pain in his belly. "I'm willing to give you another chance, but I need some time."

That wasn't what he wanted to hear, but he couldn't say he blamed her. It was his fault they were in this position, after all. If not for his leaving, they would most likely be married by now and Taylor might even have a brother or sister.

He glanced down at their naked bodies and back to her, raising one eyebrow. "So you're saying you want to take it slow?"

"Not exactly." She sighed. "I just don't want to jump in where we left off."

It was then he got it. "You don't want me to move back in."

Gabby hesitated. "I think we need to maybe test the waters first."

"So you want to date." It wasn't really a question. Besides, if he was wrong, he knew she'd correct him.

She didn't. "I think that would be the smart thing to do."

As much as he didn't want to take it slow, he understood where she was coming from. "Okay. We'll date."

A look of pure relief crossed her face and she sagged against him. "Thank you."

He tucked her head beneath his chin and cuddled her close. "Whatever you need, Gabby. I'm just grateful you're giving me another chance. I'll make it up to you. I swear I will."

"I'm going to hold you to that," she mumbled against his chest before she yawned.

"Tired?"

"Very. I didn't get much sleep last night."

He turned onto his back, taking her with him. Gabby laid her head above his chest and rested her hand on his stomach. "Sleep. We can talk more later."

"It's okay. I'm used to functioning on little to no sleep."

Jax pressed his lips to the top of her head. "I'm sorry I wasn't there to help you with Taylor."

She let out a little hum. "You help now. I've gotten more writing done in the last month than I had the previous six."

"Doesn't make up for the times I wasn't there." He trailed his fingers up and down her arm, enjoying being able to touch her freely. "Did you ever get anything published?"

He felt her nod. "Two, actually. The one I'm working on now will be number three."

"That's amazing, Gabby."

"Thanks."

She yawned again and he knew he should let her sleep. There would be time later. If the news stations were to be believed, he wasn't going anywhere until tomorrow.

"Jax?"

"Yes?" He hated to admit it, but his own lack of sleep was catching up to him. It was getting difficult to keep his eyes open.

"Did you—" She paused. "Did you date anyone when you were gone?"

That woke him up a little. He figured the topic would come up eventually, but he hadn't been prepared for it so soon. "No. No one."

She didn't comment.

The longer he lay there, the more he wondered if she had dated anyone. He had been gone three years and she was a beautiful woman. It wasn't something he wanted to think about, but given she'd brought it up . . . "What about you? Did you date anyone?"

He held his breath waiting for her to answer.

"I went on two dates with two different men."

Jax thought about the condoms in the drawer and reminded himself they hadn't been opened. As much as he wanted to ask her more, he didn't feel as if it was the right time.

She didn't seem to feel the same way. "They were both nice men. Polite. Handsome. And when I told them about Taylor they didn't get up and run in the other direction."

He was waiting for a *but*.

"At the end of the date they both asked to see me again, but I couldn't do it. My heart wasn't in it and I knew it wouldn't be fair to them if I let it continue."

The silence dragged on and he wondered if she was finished.

"You ruined me for other men."

The pattern his fingers had been making on her skin stopped. He shifted his position so he could look her in the eye. Tipping her chin up, he made sure she met his gaze. "It seems we had the same problem. I made a friend in physical therapy. He tried to fix me up a few times and I turned him down every time every time." Jax shook his head. "I couldn't imagine myself with anyone but you and, at the time, I thought I'd ruined our relationship beyond all repair."

Gabby took hold of his hand and pressed his fingers to her lips. "We're quite a pair, aren't we?"

He grinned. "So it seems."

She yawned again, but this time she rolled over, presenting him with her back.

"Are you trying to tell me something?" He'd said it as a joke, but he was being somewhat serious. If she wanted him out of her bed so she could sleep, he would go even though he didn't want to.

"That I'm sleepy?"

For a split second he thought about asking outright if she wanted him to give her some privacy, but he thought better of it. If she wasn't asking, he wasn't volunteering.

Deciding to press his luck, he eased in behind her, pressing his front to her back. He tucked one arm under his head and curled the other around her waist.

She released a contented sigh and he knew all was good. They'd make it through this. They had to. It was just going to take a little time.

***

Warmth against her back was the first thing Gabby became aware of as she awoke. The second was the sound of Jax breathing in her ear. He was still asleep. Or at least most of him was asleep. A certain part of his anatomy was very much awake and pressing into her backside. Her nipples grew hard remembering him inside her and she felt the moisture between her legs increase. As was always the case, her body was ready for him.

Gabby began edging away, knowing she needed to put some space between them before she jumped him again. She didn't get far.

"I thought you said you wouldn't run away again," Jax mumbled.

She turned to find his eyes were open, staring back at her. "I'm not. I just . . . I didn't want to wake you."

With a move swifter than she imagined possible, he reached out, wrapped an arm around her waist, and pulled her back down to lie beside him. He tucked her into his side. "That's better."

"Is it?" Her voice came out as not much more than a squeak. That wasn't good.

"Yes. We're stuck here, probably for the rest of the day, so there's no need to rush out of your nice comfy bed." He trailed his fingers down her forearm and back up to her shoulder before tracing a line along her collarbone with his index finger. "Are you hungry?"

"No. I'm fine." In reality, she wasn't fine. She wasn't sure what she was.

He nodded.

They lay there not speaking for a long time. She had to admit it was nice just being there with him. His hands never stayed still, though, and before long all her nerve endings were on fire and she was pressing her legs together looking for some friction.

"I think we need to talk some more."

His words tore her away from her more erotic thoughts. "We do?"

"Yes. I think we need to talk about where we go from here. What we want for the future."

She swallowed, not sure if she wanted to go down this path yet.

It didn't seem to matter. He plunged ahead anyway. "I understand you're not ready for us to live together again, but I'd like for that to happen. Eventually. When you're ready."

"I'm not."

He brushed a lock of her hair away from her face. "I know. And we will go as slow as you need."

Gabby pressed her lips together trying not to laugh.

"What?"

"You've been in my house for less than twenty-four hours and we've already had sex twice. I'm not sure that qualifies as slow."

He grinned. "What can I say? I'm irresistible."

Gabby punched his arm and he feigned being hurt. "Not funny."

"It wasn't meant to be a joke." He shifted his weight so she could fully feel his erection against her hip.

Unable to stop her body's reaction, she felt her pussy clench. "I thought we were going to talk."

"We are talking."

"I'm serious," she said, trying to look stern.

Jax sighed and rested his forehead on her shoulder. She heard him breath several times before he met her gaze again. "You're right. Maybe we should get dressed and check the news. If we remain here, I'm not going to able to keep my hands to myself for long."

A surge of feminine pleasure shot through her and a soft moan reverberated low in her throat.

"Gabby?"

She refocused on him and saw the look in his eyes had changed. "What?"

"If you keep making sounds like that, I'm going to forget all about being sensible."

It took her a moment to realize what he was talking about. "Sorry."

He rubbed the pad of his thumb over her lips, closed his eyes, and then climbed out of bed. Her gaze immediately went to his ass. Unlike some men, Jax had a butt—a nicely rounded one that was perfect for holding on to.

Stifling a groan, Gabby made herself stop looking and get out of bed. She walked over to the door and removed her robe from the hook. She slipped it on and turned to find Jax looking at her.

"You okay?" she asked when he continued to stare.

"Yeah." He swallowed hard. "I'm fine."

"Okay. Well, I think I'm going to go see what we have in the refrigerator and start on lunch." She wasn't hungry yet, but it would give her something to do besides jump him again.

"Sounds good." Jax picked up his discarded sweater. "If it's okay with you, I'm gonna grab a shower."

She tried not to think of him naked and wet in her shower. "Sure. You remember where everything is?"

"I'm sure I'll manage."

Neither of them budged for several seconds. Then something got him moving and he darted for the door.

Gabby waited until she heard the door to the bathroom close before she went around the room and picked up the rest of their discarded clothes. Then she made the bed. She had no idea why since they'd most likely mess it up again in the very near future, but it was something to keep her mind off what was happening in the other room.

The shower was still running when she emerged from her bedroom and made her way down the hall to the front of the house. Jax had left the television on and she stopped to see if there was anything about the weather. There wasn't. It was Saturday afternoon and as usual there was nothing on worth watching.

She picked up the remote and turned the television off before heading to the kitchen to start figuring out lunch. There was still leftover Chinese food, but she figured she'd save that for later. At the moment she needed something to keep her mind occupied.

After checking to make sure she had everything she needed, Gabby pulled out all the ingredients for her homemade lasagna. She didn't make it often because it took more time than she usually had with a three-year-old running around. Given her current situation, however, it was a perfect distraction.

Jax strolled out of the hallway ten minutes later, freshly showered. She counted her lucky stars that he was fully clothed and that he wasn't strutting around in a towel.

He spotted her and came to take a seat at the island. "What are you makin'?"

"Lasagna."

"Oh, yum." He slid off the stool and walked over to her. "How can I help?"

She was on the verge of telling him she had it covered but changed her mind. If he was busy helping her make lunch, she wouldn't have to worry so much about them ending up naked on the kitchen island. At least, that was how she rationalized it in her mind. As much as her body would have loved to do exactly that, she had to keep her head on straight. Not only for her sake, but for Taylor's as well. They couldn't afford to screw this up. Taylor didn't remember her father leaving the first time around. She would now. So Gabby had to be smart about this.

"You could brown the meat while I put the noodles on to boil."

Like no time had passed, Jax went to the drawer and pulled out her largest skillet. He picked up the package of ground meat. "The whole thing?"

"Yes, please."

Soon they were working side by side. It felt natural. Comfortable. Like he'd never left.

It took almost an hour to get everything assembled and ready to go into the oven, but it already smelled heavenly. She made sure to put a baking sheet under the casserole dish in case any of the sauce spilled over, and then shut the door.

"How long until it's done?" he asked.

"Forty-five minutes to an hour."

Jax was at the sink, rinsing off the items they'd used and loading them into the dishwasher. She'd gotten used to doing everything herself. It was nice having help again.

"Thank you."

He looked up and smiled at her. "You're feeding me. It's the least I can do."

Gabby knew she needed to come up with something or clothes were going to start coming off. She could already feel her internal temperature starting to rise. "Did you want to watch a movie? I have a few that aren't cartoons."

The soft chuckle he released stirred up the butterflies in her stomach. "Sounds good."

He held out his hand and she took it, weaving their fingers together as she led them out of the kitchen.

Chapter 9

Gabby led him into the living room and over to the bookcase where she stored their movies. "All the more adult stuff is up here."

He snorted.

"What?"

His eyes sparkled with amusement when he looked at her. "I didn't know you owned those types of movies."

It took her a moment to understand what he meant. She straightened her shoulders and looked him squarely in the eye. "So what if I did? It's not as if I've had a man around to take care of my needs."

The humor left his face and a part of her regretted snapping at him. She needed to let the past go if they were going to try and make this work.

He started to release her hand, but she held firm. "I'm sorry. I shouldn't have said that."

"It's okay. And you're right in any case."

They stood not really looking at each other or anything else for several moments, each lost in their own thoughts. "Maybe I was right, but I still shouldn't have said it." When he remained silent, she decided to try a different tactic, one she'd perfected since having a three-year-old. "Do you see a movie you want to watch?"

Jax glanced briefly at the row of maybe ten movies she had on the shelf. He selected one and held it out to her.

She took it from him and walked over to the entertainment center. Once everything was set, she picked up the remote and went to join him on the couch. He'd made sure to stay at one end, leaving plenty of room for her. Gabby considered her options. She could sit on the opposite end, letting the physical separation widen the emotional one, or she could be the bigger person and work to repair the damage she'd done to what they both had said they wanted to try and rebuild.

He met her gaze as she stood in front of him for a long moment before lowering herself down next to him. She curled her feet under her and snuggled into his side. Jax had no choice but to either put his arm around her or push her away. Luckily, he chose the first option.

As the movie played on the television, she gradually felt him begin to relax. Halfway through, she got up and removed the lasagna from the oven and fixed them both a plate. By the time the credits were rolling, their empty plates were on the coffee table and she was cuddled against his side while he played with the ends of her hair.

Gabby leaned into him and sighed. "That feels good."

"You used to like it when I played with your hair," he said, his lips ghosting along her forehead.

"I still do."

They sat there until the movie returned to the main menu. He continued to run his fingers through her hair. "I want to make it up to you, but I don't know if I can. I don't—"

She grabbed the back of his neck and brought their lips together for a hard kiss. "We'll figure it out."

"Will we?" he asked.

Releasing his neck, she lowered her hand to rest on his chest. "I hope so."

"And what if we can't?" The look on his face was full of pain. His decision to leave had hurt him, too. Not in the same way it had her, but it hurt him nonetheless.

Even still, his question was a valid one. The hurt wasn't going to go away overnight. Even if her body was more than willing to forget the past and pick up right where they'd left off, her heart still had scars that needed time to heal. "We'll figure that out, too. Taylor needs both her parents whether we're together as a couple or not. One way or another, we have to figure out how to make it work."

This time he brought their mouths together for a kiss. It was soft and breathy and had her longing for more. It was so easy to forget everything else when his lips were on hers.

"I love you," he whispered. "I want to emake you happy again . . . to see the side of your mouth lift into a smile when I walk into the room."

She lowered her gaze to his chest and then looked up at him once more. "Give me some time."

Jax nodded.

After a long pause, Gabby eased herself off the couch. She crossed the room, removed the movie from the DVD player, and put it back on the shelf. "How about a board game?"

"Sure." He stood. "What did you have in mind?"

Gabby motioned for him to follow her down the hall to the closet where she kept all the board games. Over the last year her collection had grown. Granted, most of them, like with the movies, were geared toward children. Still, it was something to pass the time. "Pick your poison."

He looked over the options and selected Candy Land.

"Really?" she asked.

"What? I used to love this game as a kid."

She laughed. "Like father, like daughter, I guess. Taylor can't get enough of it. We have to play at least once a week."

Jax smiled, and she was glad to see the melancholy of a few minutes ago had gone. He carried the box to the dining room table. While he set everything up, she retrieved their empty plates from the living room and put the rest of the lasagna away.

Two hours and several games of Candy Land later, Gabby threw up her hands. "I give up. You're cheating. You have to be."

Her accusation was said in jest, and the huge grin on his face said he hadn't taken offense. "I told you I loved this game. I could play it blindfolded."

Before she could respond, the phone rang and she got up to answer it. "Hello?"

"Are you all right?" Her sister's voice was full of worry.

"I'm fine. Why?"

She heard Grace release a loud breath. "Our electricity has been out for over an hour and I know you're alone this weekend."

Gabby glanced over at Jax, who was gathering up the game and putting it back into the box. "The electricity is still on and I'm not alone."

"Oh. I thought Taylor went to Kansas City with her grandparents. Did they cancel because of the storm?"

In for a penny, in for a pound. Besides, her sister would know soon enough that Gabby and Jax were giving it another go. "No. They left on Friday afternoon. As far as I know, they're still planning to head back home tomorrow."

"So who—"

Gabby waited for her sister to put the pieces together.

"Jax?"

"Yeah."

It took her sister a moment to respond. "How long has he been there?"

Again, Gabby's gaze drifted to Jax who had bent over to pick up something off the floor. His jeans hugged his ass, making her insides clench with want. "He came over Friday night to talk."

"And just how much *talking* have you two been doing?" By the tone of her sister's voice, she knew what Grace was really asking.

"Everything okay?" Jax mouthed to her from across the room. She could only imagine the look on her face.

Gabby nodded and went back to talking to her sister. "We've done quite a bit of talking, actually."

"I bet you have."

Grace giggled and Gabby rolled her eyes. Not all that long ago, hearing such carefree sounds from her sister would have been a rare occurrence. "What has Alexander done to my timid little sister?"

"Um . . ."

"Forget I said anything. I don't want to know."

Grace laughed. "You probably don't."

Shaking her head, Gabby decided to shift the conversation back to where it had begun. "You said your electricity was out. Do you and Alexander have everything you need? I don't know if the roads are any better than last night, but you could stay here if you need to."

"We're good for now. Alexander made a fire in the fireplace and we have bottled water and some canned food. We'll be okay for a little while." She paused. "Besides, we wouldn't want to interrupt your talking."

Speaking of talking. "Have you talked to Mom today?"

"Yeah. I called her before I called you. She said the lights flickered off and on a few times, but she never lost power. We're just lucky, I guess." Gabby heard a muffled voice in the background. "I should probably let you go."

"Alexander wants your attention, does he?"

Grace giggled. "Something like that."

"Call me if you guys change your mind about coming over," Gabby said.

"We will." And then her sister was gone.

Gabby shook her head as she put the phone down.

***

"Everything okay?" Jax asked as she strolled toward him.

"Grace was just calling to see if we had lost power. Apparently theirs went out about an hour ago." Gabby reached for the game box and tucked it under her arm. "She wanted to make sure I was all right since I was supposed to be alone this weekend."

He started to say something but stopped himself. It wasn't any of his business what she told her sister. If Gabby wanted Grace to know he was there that was her call.

"I told her we still had power." She hesitated. "And that I wasn't alone."

"What did she have to say about that?" Jax asked, trying to keep his tone casual.

"She thinks we've spent the entire time in bed."

Jax snorted. "Well, not the entire time."

Gabby smacked his arm, turned on her heel, and headed down the hallway. He followed her and watched as she returned the game to the shelf in the closet. When she spun around, Jax was there, a foot away, leaning against the wall.

He ran his hand down the length of her arm until his fingers tangled together with hers. "Why does she think we've spent the entire weekend in bed?"

The muscles in her neck contracted as she swallowed. "Because."

"Because why?" He stepped closer, crowding her. That little vein in her neck pulsed harder—a telltale sign of the effect he had on her.

Her voice cracked a little when she answered. "Because I told her what happened between us."

Jax wrapped his free arm around her waist, pressing her body against his, and she melted against him. "When you came over to my apartment to pick up Taylor?"

"Yes."

"I don't remember you and your sister being that close," he said, trying to ignore his growing erection. It didn't matter that it had been less than five hours since he'd been inside her. He wanted her again. He always wanted her. Jax wasn't sure that would ever change. In fact, he hoped it wouldn't.

She rested her hands on his shoulders as if she were steadying herself or about to push him away. "We've gotten a lot closer since she moved back."

"After her husband was killed." Taylor had mentioned something about her Aunt Grace's boyfriend one day and he'd asked his mom if she'd known anything about it. That was when he'd found out that while he'd been gone, Grace's husband, who'd been serving overseas, had been killed in combat. He'd only met Kurt once, but he liked him. And as far as Jax could tell, Kurt had loved his wife.

Sadness filled Gabby's eyes and she nodded. "Grace was a mess for a while. I was really worried about her."

He didn't like seeing her sad. "But she's better now, right?"

The tiniest smile pulled at Gabby's lips. "She is. Thanks to Alexander."

"Sounds like he was exactly what she needed." Jax lowered his hand to cup her ass, unable to resist bringing them closer. The talk of Grace losing her husband reminded Jax of his second chance with Gabby. He wasn't going to take it for granted.

"Yes." By the look in her eyes, Gabby could feel the hard length of him pressing against her abdomen.

"Maybe the four of us could go out sometime. I'd like to meet him."

"Sure." She seemed distracted.

Her gaze drifted to his mouth and he cleared his throat. "Gabby."

She placed a finger over his lips. "The food is put away and we have the house all to ourselves. I think I'd like to spend a little more time in bed."

It was his turn to swallow hard.

When he didn't respond, Gabby reached between them and cupped him through his jeans. "I know you want to."

There was no sense in denying it. She was holding the evidence in the palm of her hand. "I always want to."

A sly grin spread over her face. Gabby gave him a little squeeze and released him. She took a step backward, grabbed both his hands, and led them into the bedroom.

She wasn't wasting any time this go around. Gabby kicked off her pants and removed her shirt seconds after they entered the room. She climbed onto the bed, her ass drawing his attention like a moth to a flame.

His libido took over. Jax practically ripped his sweater in his haste to get it over his head. His jeans and boxers followed his sweater to the floor, and then he joined her on the bed. She opened herself to him, spreading her legs wide. He took a moment to appreciate the sight before him before lowering himself to cover her body with his.

Gabby circled her legs around his waist, urging him closer. He brought their lips together, dipping his tongue into her mouth, licking and exploring. "I've missed kissing you." He kissed her again, long and slow to drive the point home.

She hummed and scraped her nails along his scalp. That was new. He must have hesitated for a split second because she stopped doing it and asked, "Something wrong?"

He shook his head. "No. It's just you've never done that before. With your nails."

"Oh." She looked slightly embarrassed. "I read it in a book and I wanted to try it. If you don't like it—"

"No," he said, wanting to reassure her. "I like it." In truth, he liked it a lot.

Gabby grinned.

"Research?" She'd started writing romance novels when she'd gotten pregnant. On the nights when she couldn't sleep, she'd read the romance novels she loved so much. Then she'd gotten an idea for one of her own and, after telling him about it, he'd encouraged her to try her hand at writing one. What was the worst that could happen? And no one said she had to publish it.

She pressed her lips together and nodded.

A slow smile spread across his face and he leaned in to coax her lips apart again. "What else have you been researching?"

He ran a hand up her side and palmed her breast, skimming his thumb over her hard nipple. She arched her back, silently begging for more. Who was he to refuse her?

Sliding down, he captured her nipple in his mouth and sucked.

This time she wasn't so silent. The sweetest sound, almost like a purr, escaped her lips. His cock twitched. He did it again and her legs squeezed his middle, securing him to her.

Not that he had plans to go anywhere anytime soon. He gave the nipple a final lick before switching to give the other one the same attention. "I'm still waiting."

"What?" she asked, confused.

He sucked her nipple into his mouth, licked several times, and released it to gaze up at her beautifully flushed face. "I asked you what else you've been researching."

Her face got even redder, something he wouldn't have thought possible.

Intrigued, Jax pushed himself up until his face was level with hers again. "You're embarrassed?"

She didn't say anything. She wasn't even looking at him.

"Do I need to tickle it out of you?" he asked, trying to ease her fears. Was she afraid he'd judge her or something?

"Roll onto your back."

It was his turn to be confused. "What?"

Gabby pushed at his shoulders. "You said you wanted to know what else I'd researched. Roll over."

The idea of changing position didn't appeal to him, but he was curious what she would do. She unhooked her legs from around his middle and he moved to lie beside her.

Ever so slowly, Gabby sat up and moved until she was in between his legs. She wrapped her right hand around his cock, pumped it several times, and then took him into her mouth.

His head fell back and he tangled his fingers in her hair. *Fuck, that felt good.* It had been too long since he'd felt her lips on him.

She licked and sucked, circling his head with her tongue. His balls felt heavy. If she kept it up, he was going to come.

But as great as it was, nothing she was doing was new. The thought crossed his mind moments before he felt her free hand cup his testicles. Her touch was gentle. It was almost as if she were massaging them.

Jax clenched his fist and she released a low moan. It took him longer than it should have to realize what he'd done to cause such a reaction from her. He did it again, this time deliberately giving her hair a slight pull.

She released another soft moan that vibrated over his cock as she continued to move up and down along his length.

He was contemplating doing it again when she shifted her hand lower and began rubbing right behind his balls. Energy shot through him, and before he knew what was happening, he was on the verge of coming.

"Gabby."

She sucked harder and began a steady hum.

It was too much. His orgasm shot up his cock with a force he hadn't experienced in years.

Gabby didn't release him from her mouth until he was empty. Then she crawled up his body, grinning like the cat that ate the canary. "So? What did you think?"

She looked so innocent staring down at him like that. As if she hadn't just had those lips of hers wrapped around his cock.

He cupped the side of her face with one hand and pulled her down until her mouth was a breath away from his. "I don't know. I think I might need another demonstration."

Chapter 10

Taylor had called around seven thirty Saturday night to say good night—first to Jax and then to Gabby. It was kind of an unspoken agreement not to mention they were together. They'd each spent about five minutes talking to their daughter, listening to her tell them about her day at the children's museum. While she'd sat in bed talking to their daughter, Jax had lain there patiently beside her with a huge grin on his face.

After saying goodbye to Taylor, Jax and Gabby had lain in bed talking and touching for several hours until she could barely keep her eyes open. She'd finally asked him more about the mass they'd found, how it had been removed, and his recovery. He'd been alone for the most part. His choice, of course, but that didn't stop her from imagining him lying in a hospital bed with no one there to comfort or support him.

Gabby woke early the next morning feeling rested and more at peace than she'd felt in a long time. She knew part of it was because she was finally getting answers to the questions that had been plaguing her for the last three years.

"Good morning." Jax wrapped his arm around her waist and snuggled against her from behind.

"Hmm." She could feel his erection nudging against her backside.

He ran the tip of his nose along the column of her neck, causing her to shiver. "Sleep well?"

"Very." She tilted her head to the side to give him better access. "I liked having you in my bed."

"I like being in your bed."

Gabby felt teeth scrape against her skin, sending liquid warmth directly to her pussy. He was barely touching her and yet she knew it wouldn't take much to send her over the edge.

She reached for his hand and guided it between her legs. He let her direct the movements, caressing her sensitive flesh and driving her closer to orgasm.

Opening her legs wider, he pushed two fingers inside her. "Do you like that, baby?"

"Yes."

Jax turned them slightly, capturing her lips with his as she thrust his fingers in and out of her. "Do you want to come on my fingers or my cock?"

It took a moment for her brain to register what he said, but once she did there was no question in her mind. "Your cock. I want to come on your cock. I want you inside me."

He kissed her again and removed his fingers so he could reach into the nightstand for a condom.

Gabby squeezed her thighs together, anticipation gathering in her belly.

Luckily, he was back in seconds and wasted no time getting into position. She moaned as he entered her, filling her in a way his fingers never could.

"This what you wanted?" he asked, his voice strained.

She reached for him, needing to feel his mouth on hers again. "Exactly what I wanted."

They moved together, sensations building as she once again came to the top of that peak. She didn't wait for him this time. Gabby snaked her hand between them and found her clit.

Her orgasm hit her hard and fast. She gasped, ripping her mouth away from his.

"I love watching you." He was breathing hard, pumping into her with purpose. "Seeing your face when you come . . ."

Jax thrust into her twice more before his orgasm overtook him as well.

He collapsed on top of her, burying his face in her neck. After a few moments, he propped himself up on his elbow and stared down at her. "Care to join me for a shower?"

"I don't know if that's such a good idea."

"Why not?"

She skimmed her fingers over his ass. "Because we might not end up getting clean if we both shower together."

A wicked smirk crossed his face. "Don't worry about that. I'll make sure every inch of you is clean. Promise."

Their shower took about twice as long as Gabby's usual morning shower. He'd kept his word, though. By the time they turned off the water and dried themselves, every inch of her had been cleaned. More than once.

Jax stayed for breakfast, polishing off the breakfast casserole he'd made the day before, and then gave her a long kiss goodbye before walking out the door, promising to call her later. Because he hadn't known he was going to be stuck at Gabby's, he hadn't brought his laptop with him, which meant he couldn't work. From some of the emails he was telling her about, he was going to be very busy for the next day or so trying to catch up.

Once he was gone, she spent the rest of her morning doing laundry and tidying up. She made sure to empty the trash can in her bedroom. The last thing she wanted was her daughter discovering the used condoms Jax had discarded. That was a conversation she was hoping to put off for several more years.

They'd talked a little more about Christmas before he left. He wanted them to spend the holiday together, and even though they'd agreed to give things between them another shot, she wasn't ready to commit to anything else quite yet. A weekend fling was one thing. Spending Christmas together felt like a much bigger step.

Putting that out of her mind, Gabby concentrated on what she needed to do today. She was due at her mom's house at one for dinner, but until then she planned to do some writing. Not only did she have a book to finish, but she needed to work out some of her emotions. There was no better way to do that than to sit down and write. Writing had helped her through her pregnancy, being a first-time mom, heartbreak, and everything else life threw at her . . . even a bad day at work.

Gabby booted up her computer and opened the story she'd been working on. The first thing she did was read over what she'd written in the early hours of Saturday morning. She'd been afraid her anger would have colored her words so much that it would be out of sync with the rest of the narrative, but the exact opposite was true. The scene was full of drama and action, and when she read it, it was almost as if she could see the entire thing happening in her mind.

Her fingers flew against the keyboard as she picked up the story where she'd left off. It was almost finished. All that was left was the aftermath of the battle and the reunion of the two main characters. It would be emotional and passionate.

The sound of her cell ringing drew her attention away from the computer. She picked up her phone and answered it. "Hello?"

"Where are you?" Grace asked.

"Home." She didn't understand why her sister sounded panicked.

She heard a loud breath being released on the other end of the phone. "You're okay?"

"Of course I'm okay. Why? What's wrong?"

"What's wrong? It's two o'clock and you were supposed to be here at one."

For the first time since sitting down at her computer, Gabby looked at the clock. It was in fact two o'clock. She'd been writing for almost three hours. "I'm sorry. I was working on something and lost track of time. I'll be there in ten minutes."

Gabby saved her story and rushed out the door as quickly as possible. Luckily, the roads weren't too bad. She had to take her time at intersections, but for the most part the salt crews had gotten rid of the ice.

When she arrived at her mom's house, the door was unlocked. She stepped inside, removed her coat, and went in search of her sister. On the drive over, Gabby had had time to think about her sister's phone call. She'd hated the uncertainty and pain in Grace's voice and she wanted to apologize in person for scaring her.

"Hey, everyone," Gabby said when she strolled into the living room a few seconds later. Her mother was sitting on the couch, while Alexander and Grace were on the smaller love seat.

Caroline Lewis stood to greet her oldest daughter. "There you are. We were getting worried."

"I know." Gabby frowned. "I lost track of time. I'm sorry I worried you."

In an instant, her mother shifted gears, putting Gabby's absence behind them. "Are you hungry? I made a plate for you before we put everything away."

"Starving." And she was. The breakfast she'd had with Jax had been hours ago.

Her mom smiled and patted Gabby's forearms. "I'll go get it warmed up for you."

"Mom, I can get it."

But it was too late. Caroline was already walking away.

Gabby turned to face her sister and Alexander. His face was unreadable, but Grace's was not. It was a mixture of curiosity and concern. Crossing the room, Gabby lowered herself down onto the edge of the couch, closest to Grace. "I'm sorry."

"Are you sure you're okay? Between the storm and . . ." Grace glanced at the doorway leading to the kitchen, and then back to Gabby. "Jax, I didn't know if something had happened."

The lead-in was there and for once Gabby did want to talk about it, but this wasn't the time. Their mother could walk in at any minute and she wasn't ready to open that can of worms. Sure enough, Caroline popped her head into the living room. "Food's ready. Did you want to eat at the table, or would you rather me bring it in here?"

Pushing herself off the couch, Gabby headed toward her mom. "I'll eat at the table." She looked over her shoulder at her sister.

No words were spoken, but Grace seemed to get the message. She turned to Alexander. "Mom said she needed help fixing that rod in her closet."

Luckily, Alexander quickly picked up what was going on. "That sounds like a great idea." He stood. "Caroline, why don't we see if we can get your closet situation taken care of while Gabby eats her lunch?"

Caroline looked at both her daughters and nodded. "Sure. It's in the spare bedroom."

"Lead the way."

The two disappeared down the hall and Gabby and Grace made their way into the kitchen. Gabby grabbed the plate of food her mother had left on the counter and brought it over to the table.

Grace allowed her a couple of bites before diving in. "Are you sure you're okay?"

"I'm fine." Gabby shoveled another forkful of food into her mouth, chewed, and swallowed before continuing. "Jax and I are going to give it another try."

Her sister's eyes went wide. "As in . . ."

"As in, we're going to try being a couple again."

"Wow." Grace took a moment to gather her thoughts. "I mean, wow. Are you sure that's what you want?"

"Yes." Gabby paused. "No. I don't know."

Grace snorted.

"I know. And that's the problem." Gabby kept her voice low. "I thought I'd gotten over him, put my feelings for him behind me. But then he came back and . . ."

"And you slept with him."

"Yeah." Gabby slumped in her chair and pushed her food around with her fork. "But it's not just the sex. I . . . I still love him. And as mad as I was—I am—at him for leaving, that doesn't change the fact that even now, in the back of my mind, I'm thinking about when I'll see him again."

Her sister was silent for a minute or two and Gabby took the time to finish her food. She rinsed her plate in the sink and loaded it into the dishwasher before returning to the table.

"You don't want Mom to know," Grace said. It was a statement, not a question, although Gabby heard the other unasked questions behind it.

"No. Not until I figure this out. I told him we could try, but that doesn't mean I'm not terrified he will break my heart all over again."

Grace placed her hand on top of Gabby's. "Did he say why he left?"

"He thought he was dying."

"What?" The shock of her response came out louder than Grace had intended. "Sorry. I just . . . what?"

"He found out he had a mass on his spine or pressing against his spine or something. He kept getting these headaches and apparently that was why."

"So why didn't he tell you what was going on?"

Gabby tried not to let the anger she still felt take over. "He says he did it to protect me and Taylor. That he didn't want to put us through watching him die, or even having to go through months or years of physical therapy."

"Bullshit."

That made Gabby laugh. It wasn't often her sister cursed. "Alexander is rubbing off on you."

A blush crept up her sister's neck. "Maybe. But that doesn't make it less true."

"I know. Which is why I'm still ticked."

Movement in the living room let them know they were about to get interrupted. "If you need to talk, you know where I am."

"Thanks." Gabby stood and gave her sister a hug. "I'm glad you moved back to St. Louis. And I'm glad you found Alexander."

A few moments later, both Alexander and their mother ambled into the room. Gabby and Grace stepped apart. Their mother gave them a quick once-over again and went to the refrigerator. "Who wants some pistachio fluff?"

***

It was almost six by the time Gabby left her mom's house. Kathy Brooks had called about a half hour ago to let her know they were home. She and Nate were going to feed Taylor dinner and then drive her home.

Gabby pulled into her driveway, turned off the engine, and carried in the leftovers her mom sent home with her. She wouldn't have to worry about cooking tonight, or probably tomorrow at lunch either. There was more than enough food.

About fifteen minutes after she walked in the door, she heard a car pull up. She turned off the news and went to answer the door.

Taylor was happy, but she looked as if she was about ready to drop. Kathy gave Taylor a kiss on the cheek and handed her off to Gabby. "She woke up early this morning, so we did a little sightseeing before we left. She drifted off a few times in the car on the way back and was doing pretty good until we ate dinner."

"Her bedtime isn't that far off anyway. Thanks for feeding her," Gabby said as Taylor wrapped her arms around her mother's neck and rested her head on Gabby's shoulder. Her daughter was tuckered out.

"No need to thank me. She's our granddaughter." Kathy reached out to brush the back of her hand over Taylor's cheek. "We'll see you next weekend, sweetheart."

Taylor nodded but didn't say anything. She really was exhausted.

"Call me if you need anything," Kathy said to Gabby as she opened the door to leave.

"I will."

Once Kathy left, Gabby carried Taylor into her bedroom. She deposited her backpack on the floor in the corner—she'd deal with that tomorrow—removed a pair of clean underwear and pajamas from her daughter's dresser, and headed for the bathroom. Something told her that as soon as her daughter's head hit the pillow tonight she'd be out.

The most challenging part of Taylor's bath was trying to get her to stay awake. Normally, she loved to play with her toys, but tonight all she wanted to do was lie back and go to sleep. Gabby worked to get her body and hair washed as swiftly as possible, get her dried off, and then she tucked her into bed.

By seven thirty her daughter was asleep, which meant Gabby had the rest of the evening to herself. She decided to use the time to go over what she'd written earlier and see if any tweaking needed to be done before she sent it off to her editor.

Gabby had only gotten through the first page when her phone rang. She rushed to get it before it could wake Taylor. Although, considering how tired her daughter was, she didn't know if anything short of a freight train would rouse her sleeping child.

Her heart rate sped when she saw Jax's name on the caller ID. He said he'd call, so she shouldn't have had such a reaction, but it was there all the same. "Hi."

"Hi. Is this a good time or are you trying to get Taylor to sleep?"

"No." Gabby realized he might take that as it not being a good time. "I mean, it's a good time. Taylor's already asleep. She barely kept her eyes open during her bath."

"Mom said she was pretty tired when she dropped her off."

"She was."

They talked a little more about Taylor, and then he switched gears on her. "I was wondering if I could take you out on Wednesday night."

The breath caught in Gabby's throat, making it hard to answer. "Out?"

"Yeah. Out. As in a date. Just you and me. I already asked Mom and she said she could come by and watch Taylor if you wanted. I didn't know if your sister or your mom would be available on such short notice. And I figured you'd want someone to watch her at the house so it doesn't mess with her bedtime."

Gabby realized he was rambling, which meant he was nervous. The thought eased some of her tension. Even though she'd agreed to give them another shot, he wasn't sure she'd say yes. The slightly vindictive part of her kind of liked that he was suffering and wanted to drag it out a little. "What kind of date did you have in mind?"

"I was kind of hoping to surprise you."

"I see."

He was quiet for a few moments. "Did you change your mind? About us, I mean?"

She sighed. It was no good being petty. It wasn't going to solve anything. "No. I didn't change my mind."

"Good." Gabby could feel the relief washing over him through the phone. "So Wednesday?"

"What time?" she asked.

"I was thinking about seven. That way you and Taylor can eat together. Mom can come over a little before then, say around six forty-five."

"Sounds like a plan."

"It's a date, then," he said, a smile in his voice.

His happiness was contagious. "It's a date."

***

Gabby didn't hear from Jax again until Wednesday afternoon when he sent her a text confirming he'd be there to pick her up at seven. She'd tried not to think too much about their date or where the night might end up going. Her body was already singing with the thought of being with him again.

At six forty there was a knock on her door. Kathy greeted her with a smile and a bag of cookies for Taylor. "If you don't want her to have them tonight, I can tuck them in my purse and leave them on the counter after she goes to bed."

"No, it's fine," Gabby said as she motioned Jax's mother inside. "She ate her dinner, so she can have a cookie if she wants."

Kathy set the bag of cookies on the table and hung her coat on the back of one of the chairs. She didn't say anything about Gabby's impending date with Jax, which was good. Gabby really didn't want to talk about it.

"Taylor's playing in her room. I laid her pajamas out on her bed already and her toothbrush is on the sink in the bathroom."

Kathy smiled. "I'm sure we'll be fine. If not, I have your number. Just go have a nice time."

As if on cue, there was a knock at the door. Gabby could already feel her palms getting sweaty. She didn't know why she was so nervous. It wasn't as if they hadn't done this before.

"I'll get it," Kathy said. "Why don't you go say goodbye to Taylor?"

Happy for a couple of extra minutes to prepare herself for seeing him again, Gabby went to find her daughter. She was sitting on her bed, legs spread out in front of her, flipping through one of her favorite books. "Hey."

Taylor looked up.

"Grandma Brooks is here to watch you while Mommy and Daddy are gone."

"Okay," Taylor said, not seeming to be the least bit bothered that her mother was leaving.

Gabby walked over to the bed and gave her daughter a kiss on the cheek. "You be good for Grandma and I'll see you in the morning."

Taylor rose up on her knees, letting her book drop to the mattress, and circled her arms around Gabby's neck. Her daughter planted a loud kiss on her mother's cheek and released her. Almost immediately she reached for her discarded book again and went back to what she was doing as if nothing had happened.

Gabby chuckled and shook her head as she backed out of the room. "Love you."

Her daughter's face lit up as she stared back at her. "Loves you, too, Mommy."

She stepped out into the hallway and came face-to-face with Jax. "Everything all right?"

"Um. Yeah. I was just . . ." She gestured toward her daughter's bedroom door. "I was just saying goodbye to Taylor."

He grinned and she felt the butterflies begin to dance in the pit of her stomach. She didn't know how he did it or why her body had such a reaction to him, but she was done fighting it. "I figured I'd pop my head in and say good night before we leave."

"Okay," she said to an empty hallway.

Kathy was sitting on the couch, watching television, when Gabby walked into the main room. She switched it off and stood.

Jax appeared a few seconds later and strode toward her with all the confidence in the world. "Ready to go?"

"Sure."

He removed her coat from the closet and helped her put it on.

"Thanks."

"You're welcome." Jax opened the door and waited for her to go through it.

"Have fun," Kathy said as they walked out the door.

Jax put his hand on Gabby's lower back and the contact sent warmth through her bones. The door closed behind them and he leaned in to whisper in Gabby's ear. "Fun is guaranteed."

Chapter 11

Jax had given a lot of thought as to where to take Gabby. He'd known she'd want to have dinner with Taylor, so that was out of the question. Dessert was an option, but he wanted to do something a bit more festive.

They were almost there when Gabby figured out where they were going. "Are we going to the zoo?"

He glanced over at her and grinned as he maneuvered into the turning lane. "What? You don't like the zoo?"

"No." She shook her head. "I just wasn't expecting us to be outside for long periods of time. I would have dressed warmer."

Turning into the parking lot, Jax paid the guy in the little hut and started looking for a spot. "Don't worry about that. I promise I'll keep you nice and warm."

She didn't have any comeback to that, and he had to work hard not to laugh at the look of deep concentration on her face.

For a Wednesday night, there were quite a few people out. Then again, it was a beautiful evening. All the ice from the weekend had melted as milder temperatures moved in. There was still a chill in the air—it was December—but they would be able to spend an hour or so walking through the zoo without being in danger of frostbite.

He bought their tickets and they made their way inside. All the trees and bushes were draped in lights for the holidays. It was beautiful.

"I haven't been here in years," Gabby said as they began to walk along the path.

"Neither have I. We'll have to bring Taylor one of these days."

Gabby smiled, the first time since he'd picked her up. "She'd love all the lights."

They stopped at the petting zoo and fed the goats. The brown one followed Gabby around. Every time she tried to feed another goat, the brown one would push the other one out of the way and snatch the food from Gabby's hand. Jax tried to keep from laughing, but it was impossible. The entire thing was too funny.

Once they were finished with the petting zoo, they continued on, stopping at each of the exhibits to see the animals and take in the lights. Even the exhibits that were empty because the animals were inside were decked out in lights.

As they strolled, they chatted about the lights, the animals, and even the weather. It was all very civilized and he was pleased to see her relax and enjoy herself. They crossed over a bridge filled with huge fish. She knelt down to get a closer look, rubbing her hands together in an effort to warm them up.

"How about some hot chocolate?" Jax asked. "I did promise to keep you warm."

She stood and shoved her hands back into her pockets. "That sounds great."

They changed direction and headed toward the food court. Jax walked up to window and ordered two hot chocolates and a soft pretzel. After paying, he guided them over to a bench and they sat down to sip their drinks. He tore off a piece of the pretzel, popped it into his mouth, and offered her some. "Having fun?"

A slight blush colored her cheeks as she pinched off a bit of the warm bread for herself. "Yes."

"Good." He was unable to hide his grin.

They sat people-watching for several minutes, not speaking and finishing off the pretzel.

"I wanted to ask you something."

He took a drink of his hot chocolate as he tried to ignore the way his pulse picked up. Was this just another way of saying 'we need to talk'? That was never a good sign. "Shoot."

Gabby rolled her cup in between her hands several times. "Where do you think we'd be right now if you hadn't left three years ago?"

"That's easy," he said without any hesitation. "We'd be married and Taylor would probably have another brother or sister."

She looked over at him, her eyebrows raised slightly. "You sound confident about that."

"Well, I already had the ring. I was just trying to find the right time to ask you."

"And the other part?"

He shrugged, unaffected by the direction the conversation had taken. "I figure nature would have taken its course with that one. It wasn't as if we ever had trouble in the bedroom."

The blush was back. This time it colored both her neck and cheeks. She glanced around, but no one was paying attention to them.

He reached over and ran the back of his hand along her jaw. Gabby shivered. "Cold?"

"No," she whispered, shaking her head.

The look in her eyes told him all he needed to know in that moment. He could feel the pull between them and needed to touch her more than he needed his next breath.

Cupping the side of her face, Jax closed the distance between them and brushed his lips against hers. He kept the kiss light and PG rated considering they were in public and there were children around, but that didn't mean he couldn't convey what he was feeling through the kiss.

She released a soft sigh when he pulled back enough to meet her gaze. He tucked a lock of hair behind her ear, unable to stop touching her.

Gabby searched his eyes as they sat there in the cool night air, surrounded by people. She scraped her teeth over her bottom lip. "You really had a ring?"

"I still have it." There was no need to deny it and, in any case, he didn't want to.

She sucked in a harsh breath. "Why?"

Jax shrugged and trailed his fingers down the side of her face. "I guess one day I was hoping I'd get to come back to you, to have the life I dreamed about."

"Where . . ."

He knew what she was asking. "The ring is in my dresser at my apartment."

The vein in the side of her neck was pulsing out of control and all he could think about was kissing it. He knew how much she liked it when he paid attention to her neck. She was so sensitive there.

Without much warning, Gabby stood, nearly knocking his hot chocolate out of his hand. She glanced around, looking flustered, and he couldn't help but feel quite pleased with himself about that.

He eased himself off the bench. "Something wrong?"

Gabby shook her head but wouldn't look at him. "No. I just thought we should probably get moving again if we're going to see the rest of the exhibits. I'm sure your mother doesn't want to be out all night."

The rest of the walk through the zoo was filled with tension—a stark contrast to how things had been before their conversation. His revelation that he'd been about to ask her to marry him and still had hopes to do so had clearly thrown her, and as much as he wanted to push her to talk to him, he was giving her some time to process what she was feeling. He was the one who'd screwed up. Not her. As hard as it was, he was going to have to let her set the pace.

"Are you hungry?" he asked as they were leaving the zoo. It was getting late, but he didn't want to say good night to her yet.

"Not really." She was looking out the window at the lights as they drove from the parking lot.

With a sigh, he headed in the direction of her house. He'd wanted this date to be a positive experience. Now he was concerned it would be the opposite.

Jax felt her gaze on him as he turned onto the highway. He waited for her to say something, but she never did.

Fifteen minutes later he pulled up in front of her house and turned off the engine. She was still watching him, but when he met her gaze it wasn't what he'd expected. He'd expected uncertainty and maybe a little fear, but instead it appeared as if she was deep in thought.

They sat in the car for several minutes before she broke the silence. "Do you want to come in?"

He didn't want to read too much into it. Besides, his mother was in there. "Sure."

Gabby was already outside the car waiting for him when he rounded the vehicle. They walked side by side, not touching, to the door and he waited for her to put her key in the lock. Jax flexed his hands, telling himself to be patient.

When they stepped into the house his mom peeked up from the book she'd been reading. She bookmarked her place, closed the novel, and stood. "You're home early."

"We didn't want to be out too late," Gabby said, taking off her coat.

"There was no rush. I made sure to bring a book to keep me company."

Gabby's attention went to the book his mother had pressed against her chest. It looked rather racy if the cover was anything to go by. He'd had no idea his mom read books like that. Then again, that wasn't exactly the type of discussion a grown man typically had with his mother.

His mom followed Gabby's gaze, and if he wasn't mistaken his mother's cheeks darkened a little. "Gabby, you like romance novels, right? Have you ever read G. E. Lewis?"

He saw Gabby shift her weight. "I believe I've heard of her."

"A friend recommended her books to me and I have to say they're hard to put down." His mom leaned toward Gabby and lowered her voice. "Not that my husband is complaining. It's put a little more zing in the bedroom, if you know what I mean."

"Mom!"

Kathy laughed. "Oh please. If your father and I never had sex, you wouldn't be here."

"While that might be the case, it doesn't mean I want to hear about it."

His mom acted as if he hadn't said a word. "Since you're home, I'll head out. Taylor went to bed around eight thirty, and when I looked in on her about nine she was sound asleep. Haven't heard a peep out of her since."

"Thank you again for watching her," Gabby said.

"Any time." His mom slipped on her coat, stuffed the book she'd been reading into her purse, and reached for the door. "I left the rest of the cookies on the counter by the sink. Taylor and I each only had one, so there are plenty left. Call me if you need me to babysit again."

***

As soon as Kathy was out the door, Gabby went to check on Taylor. She pushed the door open enough for her to poke her head in. Taylor was on her side, her favorite doll in her arms.

Gabby felt Jax come up behind her so she backed away, pulling the door closed.

"She all right?" he asked.

"Yeah. She's out like a light." Gabby forced her feet to move. She knew if they stayed there in the hall she would be tempted to drag him into her bedroom across the hall and have her wicked way with him.

Jax followed her into the living room.

Her first instinct was to straighten up, but there wasn't anything to do. The house was in great shape—better than she'd left it. Kathy had cleaned up any messes that the two of them might have made and had even fixed the throw on the back of the couch. It was too bad because Gabby could really have used the distraction.

She started to go into the kitchen and then changed her mind at the last minute.

To hell with it.

Gabby pivoted and marched over to stand directly in front of Jax. Without overthinking it, she took two fistfuls of his coat, pulled him toward her, and kissed him hard.

It took all of a second for him to get with the new program. He wrapped his arms around her body, molding her to him, holding her head exactly where he wanted it as he took control of the kiss.

Warmth spread through her limbs as the sensations overwhelmed her. She melted against him, needing more. He seemed to sense what she craved and pressed their lower bodies together, letting her feel how much he wanted her. She moaned, anticipation curling in her belly. Her body knew exactly what pleasure Jax could bring.

It was only the sound of a muffled thump that brought her out of the haze she was in. Gabby jerked away from him.

She paused, waiting to see if she'd hear it again, but all she could hear was their labored breathing.

"What is it?" he asked, picking up that something was wrong.

"I thought I heard something hit the floor."

Jax frowned. "I didn't hear anything."

To be honest, Gabby was surprised she'd heard anything either considering how caught up in the moment she'd been. "I need to check on Taylor."

Without comment, he released her.

Gabby rushed down the hall, needing to make sure her daughter was all right. She breathed a sigh of relief when she found Taylor still in bed and fast asleep. Her daughter was no longer on her side, however. She had rolled over and twisted somehow so that her feet were facing the wall. Based on her position, Gabby guessed the noise she'd heard was the sound of her daughter's foot making contact with the drywall.

Letting go of her momentary anxiety, Gabby pulled the door shut again and headed back out to where Jax waited. "I think she kicked the wall with her foot or something. She's still sound asleep, though."

He started to move toward her, the look in his eyes making it clear he had every intention of picking up where they'd left off.

Gabby decided maybe a change of direction was in order. She needed to cool off and think, and she couldn't do that when he was touching her. "I wonder what kind of cookies your mom made."

Without giving him time to adjust to her complete one-eighty, Gabby went into the kitchen and found the cookies.

She took one out of the bag and bit into it. The chocolate hit her tongue and she closed her eyes to savor the moment. Kathy had always made the best sweets.

When she opened her eyes again, Jax was staring at her. He was watching her lips, and it didn't take a genius to know what he was thinking.

Grabbing a plate, she set the cookie down and went to the refrigerator for some milk. "Want some?" she asked, holding up the gallon of milk.

"No, thanks."

She poured herself a glass and returned the jug to the refrigerator. Taking her cookie and milk over to the island, she pulled out a stool and sat down.

Jax watched her every move. He waited until she was almost finished with her cookie before sitting down on the stool beside her. "Does the thought of us getting married one day scare you?"

"No. Not really." She finished off her cookie and drank the rest of her milk. "Not once I'd had a chance to think about it."

He reached for her hand, lacing their fingers together. "Then why have you seemed so distant since our conversation on the bench?"

"I didn't know kissing you was considered being distant."

Jax chuckled and squeezed her hand. "Aside from that."

Sure, she could keep avoiding the question, but that wasn't going to help the situation. "I've been thinking."

"Okay." He squared his shoulders as if he was bracing himself for whatever it was she was about to say.

"I think we should take Taylor to the zoo to see the lights on Saturday night."

That was clearly not what he'd been expecting her to say. "All three of us?"

"Yes." Gabby swallowed. "And I was thinking about Christmas."

He'd been rubbing the inside of her wrist with his thumb, but he paused and held her gaze. "What about Christmas?"

She took a deep breath and prepared herself for what she was about to say. Several things had become clear to her in the last week. For one, she was still as much in love with Jax as she'd ever been. She wasn't sure anything was ever going to change that. He'd broken her heart and still he was the only man who could make her heart race with nothing more than a look or a touch. She was tired of fighting it—tired of trying to remind herself of all the reasons she should guard her heart.

It was useless anyway. Her heart already belonged to him. It always had.

"I think you're right. We should have Christmas together as a family."

His lips curled into a smile that lit up his face.

"And," she said before he could comment, "I think it should start here."

Jax's grin faltered a little. "You want my mom and dad to come here first?"

She shook her head. "No. I figured you and I would watch Taylor open her presents here first, and then we could go over to your parents' for dinner or something. Or maybe we could all go over to my mom's."

He sat up a little and reached for her, turning her to face him. Scooting his stool closer, he held on to her waist and situated her between his knees. His brow was furrowed, deep in concentration, as he mulled over what she'd said.

Deciding to let him off the hook, she reached out and cupped the side of his face. "That's what families do, right? They wake up on Christmas morning and open presents together?"

"You want me to spend the night on Christmas Eve so I can be here for Christmas morning?"

Gabby nodded and waited to see where his thoughts went next.

He leaned into her touch, covering her hand with his. "Don't you think that might be a little confusing for Taylor? Or are you going to make me sleep on the couch?"

"I think Taylor would be used to you spending the night by then."

Jax closed his eyes and took a deep breath before meeting her gaze again. "Sweetheart, I need for you to spell it out for me. I'm dying here."

Slipping off her stool, Gabby stepped in between his legs and wrapped her arms around his neck. "Do you promise never to leave Taylor and me again?"

"You couldn't drag me away."

"That's good." She pressed her lips to his in a barely there kiss. "I want you to move back in with us. I want to wake up with you beside me every morning. And I want to fall asleep every night knowing you're there."

"That's what I want, too." He tucked her hair behind her ear. "I love you."

"I love you, t—"

His mouth covered hers and she let herself be swept away by the kiss.

When they finally came up for air several minutes later, he'd snaked his hand up her shirt and was working his way under her bra. She needed to get out of these clothes. Pronto.

Gathering what little willpower she had left, Gabby tore her mouth away from his and backed away. Before he could protest, though, she grabbed his hand and began leading him toward the bedroom—their bedroom.

Chapter 12

"Good morning." Jax stood beside the bed, wearing nothing but a towel wrapped around his waist.

Gabby lifted her arms above her head and stretched. "Morning."

The action caused the blanket to inch lower, exposing her breasts, and his gaze followed.

His pupils dilated and her nipples began to harden in anticipation.

But they couldn't go there. Taylor would be up soon and Gabby didn't want to start the morning by trying to explain the birds and the bees.

Pulling the cover up and tucking it under her arms, she propped herself against the headboard. "You're up early."

Jax shrugged and went to the backpack he'd retrieved from the trunk of his car the night before to dig out a clean pair of jeans and underwear. "It was either get up and take a shower or ravish you again." He shot her a glance over his shoulder, his eyes still smoldering. "I decided to be a gentleman and let you sleep."

She felt her inner muscles clench and release.

"That," he said, "and we have to talk to Taylor this morning and figure out how to explain the new living arrangements."

That sobered her up. Of course they needed to talk to their daughter about Jax moving in. Gabby didn't think Taylor would have a problem with her father being here full time. In fact, she was guessing Taylor would be thrilled about it. But one could never tell with a three-year-old. Sometimes what Gabby thought wouldn't be a big deal ended up in an epic tantrum and vice versa.

Gabby threw the covers off her, got out of bed, and went to get her robe. There was no sense in getting dressed until after she'd had a shower. She smelled like sex and Jax. Not that she was complaining, but she needed to be in mom mode this morning and that meant putting her needs as a woman on the back burner.

She secured the robe around her middle and padded across the room to her dresser to get some clean clothes. When she turned around, clothes in hand, Jax was standing there looking as appealing as ever. He was dressed in dark blue jeans and a long-sleeved shirt that had her wanting to run her hands over every inch of him.

Without a word, he cradled her face in his hands and lowered his mouth to hers.

It was a simple kiss, but it left her insides tingling.

He ran his thumb along her cheek and stared into her eyes. "I'll make us some breakfast while you shower. Eggs and bacon okay?"

"Sounds perfect."

Jax grinned and gave her another quick kiss before he dropped his hand and moved away. "Don't take too long or I might be tempted to come help you."

She chuckled and headed for the door. "Somehow I doubt you'd speed things along."

His laughter filled her ears as she entered the bathroom.

Gabby hurried through her morning routine, but she was still drying her hair when a soft knock sounded on the bathroom door. "Mommy?"

She opened it to find her sleepy-eyed daughter standing on the other side in her pajamas. "Good morning, sweetheart. Did you need to go to the bathroom?"

Taylor nodded.

"Okay. I'll be outside if you need help."

After bathroom rituals were taken care of, Gabby and Taylor made their way into the kitchen where Jax was plating the eggs. He looked up at their arrival and smiled. "Perfect timing, ladies."

"Smells good."

Taylor must not have been fully awake before, because it was only when she heard her father's voice that she lit up. "Daddy! You're here."

She launched herself across the room and into his arms. "Morning, Pumpkin."

That feeling of rightness filled Gabby's chest.

"Are you hungry?" Jax asked.

Taylor nodded.

He set her on her feet and picked up the plates containing the eggs and bacon, taking them over to the table.

"Do you want milk or juice, Taylor?" Gabby asked, going to the refrigerator.

"Juice, please."

"Jax?"

"Juice works for me, too." He shot her a grin before he sat down.

After pouring everyone some juice, Gabby sat down at the table and they all began to eat the food Jax had prepared. About halfway through, Jax and Gabby looked at each other. It was time to address the elephant in the room.

Gabby dove in. "Taylor? What do you think of Daddy being here this morning? Do you like having him here eating breakfast with us?"

The reaction from Taylor was unmistakable. Her eyes sparkled and she nodded as she chewed on her bacon.

"How would you feel about Daddy living with us?"

Taylor thought about it for a moment. "Would Daddy have breakfast with us every morning?"

Jax answered. "Yes. That means I'd have breakfast with you and Mommy every morning."

"Okay."

She went back to eating her food as if one of the most pivotal conversations of Gabby's life hadn't just happened. It had to be one of the easiest conversations she'd ever had in her life.

After breakfast, Jax cleaned up while Gabby got Taylor ready for preschool. She had to say it was nice having another adult around to help. Cleaning up the kitchen was one less thing she had to worry about before leaving the house.

"Ready for preschool?" Jax asked when they emerged from Taylor's bedroom.

She hoisted her backpack on her shoulders. "Are you taking me to school, too, Daddy?"

"Not today. I have a meeting this morning." At her disappointed look, he added, "Maybe I can take you tomorrow."

That cheered her up. "I can introduce you to Mrs. Von. She's really nice."

He ran a hand over the top of her head. "I can't wait."

Jax gave her a hug and a peck on the cheek then turned to Gabby. She saw so many things in his eyes as he looked at her—things that made her wish they didn't have an audience. "I'll see you tonight. If you need me or can't find something, you have my cell. And there's an extra key in the nightstand beside my bed."

"I'm sure I'll be fine." He took hold of her free hand and brought it to his mouth, letting his lips linger on her skin. "Have a good day at work, honey."

She laughed, breaking some of the tension. "Thanks. You, too."

The rest of the day seemed to drag since all she wanted to do was be home with Jax. Gabby kept wondering what he was doing. She must have thought about calling him at least a dozen times, but she'd resisted. He'd call if he needed something.

When she walked in the front door later that evening with Taylor, Jax was sitting on the couch, glasses on, his feet propped up on the coffee table, and his laptop resting on his lap.

Neither Jax nor Gabby got a word out, however, before Taylor was running across the room and jumping onto the couch beside him. He almost dropped his laptop on the floor when she plopped onto his lap and threw her arms around him.

Gabby chuckled as she removed her coat and hung it up in the hall closet. It didn't seem as though their daughter would have any trouble adjusting to her father being there all the time.

That night after putting Taylor to bed, Gabby tidied up the house while Jax loaded the dishwasher. In some ways, it was as if no time had passed and they'd picked up where they'd left off three years ago. Could it really be that simple?

"I stopped by my apartment earlier and picked up enough clothes to last me till Saturday," Jax said as he wiped off the counter.

She straightened the rug by the front door and joined him in the kitchen. "Do you think your mom would want to watch Taylor Saturday while we get you moved?"

He stopped what he was doing and focused on her. "Are you ready for that?"

"I asked you to move in, didn't I?"

"Yes. But if you'd rather me keep the apartment for a while, I can. There's no rush." He made sure he was looking her in the eye when he said, "I'm not going anywhere."

For the first time, she didn't have that voice in the back of her head pinging her with doubts. "I know. And, yes, I'm ready. If I wasn't, I wouldn't have asked you in the first place. Taylor needs stability. It would be confusing for her if you moved in one day and then moved out the next."

Jax hung the dish towel on the front of the oven and came to stand in front of her. The look in his eyes was full of love—a love that her heart echoed. He took both her hands and began walking backward, toward the bedroom.

"Where're we going?" she asked.

"To bed."

"We should turn off the lights, then."

He looked around and nodded. "You're right."

As swiftly as he could, he ran to every light and switched it off before returning to her. But this time, he picked her up and swung her around. "Now, where were we?"

Gabby giggled. "I do believe you said we were heading to bed."

"Ah. Yes. Bed." With that, he swung her up into his arms and carried her down the hall toward their bedroom. She had to bite her lip to keep from laughing. She didn't want to wake Taylor.

***

Bright and early Saturday morning, they dropped Taylor off at Jax's parents' house and drove to his apartment to pack things up. He'd already started loading the boxes during his trips home over the last two days, so there wasn't all that much to pack. It didn't take more than a few hours to gather up his belongings and load them into his vehicle.

They headed back to her house—what would now be their house—and carried the boxes inside. As they were sorting through his things and putting them away, Gabby noticed he had very few books, a huge contrast to when he'd left. Jax used to have an extensive science fiction collection. She broke down the box she'd been working on, the last one apart from the one Jax was unpacking, and asked, "What happened to all your books?"

He looked up at her for a brief moment and then went back to what he was doing. "I gave most of them to a community center."

"Why would you do that?" He'd loved his books. She couldn't understand why he'd given them away.

"I was in a rehab facility for a while after my surgery. It didn't make sense to keep them when I didn't really have a place for them. I kept five of my favorites. The rest I gave away." There was sadness in his voice and she didn't know if it was because of the books he'd given up or because recalling that time in his life caused him as much pain as it did her.

Not wanting to go there again, even though that's exactly where her mind went, she turned her attention to his clothes that they'd draped over the bed. Going to her closet, she moved everything to one side, creating room. "Do you think this will be enough space for you?"

Jax walked over to where she stood. He put his arms around her waist, pulling her back against him. "I don't have all that much to hang up, so I'm sure it'll be fine."

She nodded as the heat from his body already had her girl parts standing at attention.

"Why don't we take a break and go grab some lunch? All this work has made me hungry."

Twisting around so she could face him, Gabby stood on her tiptoes to give him a soft yet lingering kiss on the lips. "I've worked up quite an appetite as well."

By the tone of her voice it was obvious she wasn't talking about food. Jax closed his eyes and groaned. "You're killing me."

"What? Not in the mood?" She stared up at him with a mischievous look on her face.

He opened his eyes again and backed her against the nearest wall. Pressing their lower bodies together, she could feel every inch of him against her belly. "I think you'll agree that's not an issue."

She reached for the button on his jeans.

His hand covered hers, halting her movements. "Tell me what you were thinking about before."

Gabby knew what he was referring to and it wasn't how much she wanted him. As much as she didn't want to talk about it, she knew if they had any hope of making this relationship work long term they couldn't keep secrets. That was what had gotten them in trouble the last time. His secrets. But that didn't matter at this point. She'd agreed to move forward. "I hadn't thought about what it was like for you when you left."

Her voice cracked on the last syllable.

Jax ran his hand up the side of her arm and back down again. She knew it was meant to be comforting, but all it did was stoke the fire that was already stirring in her belly. "I don't want you to hurt for me. I've caused you enough pain already."

Placing a hand on his chest, she held his gaze. "If we're going to move past this, then we're going to have to forgive each other. And you're going to have to forgive yourself. Otherwise, this isn't going to work."

He covered her hand with his and gave it a gentle squeeze. "When did you become so wise?"

"Hmm." Gabby looked up at the ceiling as though she were contemplating something profound. "I don't know." She looked him in the eye again, the heaviness of the previous moment's mood gone. "It just sort of happened."

Then he was tickling her. She gasped for air as she tried to get out of his reach.

He pinned her against the wall with his body and captured her mouth with his own. A sigh escaped her throat as any thought about trying to get away fled from her mind. She sank into the kiss, letting her tongue mingle with his as he cupped her ass and lifted both her legs to encircle his waist.

The next thing she knew, they were moving. Seconds later, she fell onto the mattress.

They were both breathing hard as he peered down at her, his eyes less troubled than she'd seen them since he'd been back. "I love you."

Her chest clenched. She would never get tired of hearing him say that. Especially since she thought she'd never hear it again.

Gabby reached for him, pulling him down until his lips were a breath away from hers. She looked at his mouth and then in his eyes. "We have to make this work."

His elbows were braced on either side of her head as he held his position with their lips so close yet not quite touching. "We will. We'll make sure of it."

There was no doubt he believed every word he was saying, and for maybe the first time, she believed it, too. The future wasn't so scary. Not if they were in it together.

"I think we should get married."

He froze above her.

It took a full thirty breaths for him to respond. She knew because she'd counted. Counted and waited with growing anxiety to see how he'd react. He'd said he wanted to marry her in the future, but maybe he'd meant far into the future. Maybe—

"I thought you said you wanted to wait a while . . . have us try living together again first."

She lifted one shoulder, or at least tried to given their position. It was kind of hard to shrug when they were pressed together from chest to hip. "I changed my mind."

Jax was quiet, his brow furrowed. She knew he was thinking. What if he said no?

"When?"

"What?" She'd been so focused on what was going on inside her own head that his question threw her off.

He didn't seem the least bit fazed by her question. "When do you want to get married?"

"Um. I don't know. I hadn't really thought about it." She didn't want anything fancy. Something small with their friends and family would be perfect in her opinion. "What about Christmas Eve?"

"As in next week Christmas Eve?" he asked.

"Yeah." She paused. "Unless you think it's too soon."

A slow smile spread across Jax's face. "Not at all. I'd marry you tomorrow. Today, even. I just always thought you'd want a big wedding. The dress. The cake."

Gabby shook her head. "I don't want any of that. All I want is you, our daughter, our family and a few friends."

His fingers played with the hair near her temples. "I think that sounds perfect."

"So I guess that means we're engaged." She went to pull him closer to seal their engagement with a kiss, but he began to move away. "Where—"

"Hold on. I need to get something." He went over to the backpack he had sitting in the corner—the one he'd been ferrying his clothes back and forth in for the last two days—and began rummaging through it.

She propped herself up on her elbows so she could see what he was doing.

"Got it," he said and returned to the bed.

Instead of climbing back onto the mattress with her, he stood off to the side and reached to help her sit up. It was then she saw he had a small box in his hand and realization dawned.

With her sitting on the edge of the bed, Jax took her left hand and knelt down on one knee. "Gabrielle Lewis, would you do me the honor of becoming my wife?"

Gabby couldn't contain her smile. She should have known Jax would want to propose to her properly. "Yes."

Jax opened the box, revealing a simple ring with three diamonds. He beamed as he slipped it onto her ring finger.

"It's beautiful."

He threaded his fingers through her hair at the back of her neck and brought her in for a kiss.

She went willingly, the feel of the ring on her finger at the forefront of her mind. And as his lips shifted to her neck, all the implications of what they'd talked about started to form even as her body was becoming more and more aroused. "We'll need to find a place to have the wedding."

Grabbing the hem of Gabby's sweater, he began inching it up her torso and over her head. "Uh-huh."

"Maybe we could have it at your parents' house. Or if they'd rather not, we could have it here."

He released the clasp of her bra and nudged the straps off her shoulders.

"I wonder if we will be able to find a minister at such short notice."

"Gabby?"

She looked down at him. His eyes were dancing with amusement.

He cupped one of her breasts and began to massage it, sending a jolt of electricity to her core. "Can we talk about this later?"

"Sorry. All these things started popping into my head."

Jax stood. "And we'll figure it all out. I promise." He lifted her and tossed her farther back onto the bed. "Right now I'd really like to make love to my beautiful fiancée."

Before she could think of anything else to say, he'd joined her on the bed, his mouth latching on to one of her nipples and his hand snaking its way into her jeans to stroke her. Later suddenly sounded like a very good idea.

Epilogue

Jax stood in front of the large fireplace at his parents' house, listening to his dad and Alexander talk about some new drug that was on the market. He was only half paying attention as their family and friends filled up his parents' living room. They'd borrowed some chairs and set them up in the living room for people to sit on during the small ceremony, and almost all of them were full.

His dad had built a fire earlier that morning to warm the room. It was a good thing, too, since every time the front door was opened cold air wafted in from outside and crept into the living room. Not that Jax needed the extra heat. He was sweating under his suit and it had nothing to do with the temperature in the room. He was nervous, plain and simple. Not about marrying Gabby—he couldn't wait for that—it was more that he wanted this day to be perfect for her and was afraid this rushed wedding wasn't going to live up to her expectations.

He had no rational reason to think that, however. Gabby had insisted a small wedding was exactly what she wanted. She didn't want to wait the year or so it would take to pull off something more extravagant. In her mind, they'd wasted enough time and, in that respect, he couldn't disagree with her. They had wasted too much time and it was entirely his fault.

Pushing the self-loathing aside, he focused on the present. Gabby had been right when she said they both needed to forgive each other and themselves. Living in the past didn't solve anything and would only hinder their future.

Thanks to both of their mothers, they'd somehow managed to put together a wedding in a little over a week. They'd both fully embraced Jax and Gabby's engagement and jumped in with both feet to help however they could. He still wasn't sure how they'd done it. All the talk of cakes and decorations and seating had made his head spin.

His gaze fell on the Christmas tree a few feet away. Usually his parents' Christmas tree was decorated with various ornaments from his childhood. But since this was a special occasion, his mom had insisted the tree needed to look the part. It was covered in a mixture of silver, gold, red, and white and looked as if it had come right out of a magazine.

A flash of red caught his attention and he zeroed in on it. The sound of female laughter filtered in from the hall a moment before Grace moved into his line of sight.

The only family member who'd been a bit skeptical was Grace. When they'd told Gabby's mother, Caroline, she'd just smiled and said she knew it would all work out eventually. Grace, however, had looked at them both as if they'd lost their minds. He knew it was out of fear he'd break her sister's heart again, and to be honest, he couldn't blame her. It wasn't as if he didn't deserve her skepticism.

In an effort to mend fences, Jax, Gabby, Grace, and Alexander, whom Jax was still trying to get to know, all went out to dinner two nights ago to clear the air. He wasn't sure everything was peachy keen now, but at least he was confident Grace knew his intentions when it came to Gabby and Taylor were honorable.

Grace strolled into the living room holding Taylor's hand. His daughter looked adorable in her fancy dress—the perfect little flower girl. He only hoped her dress made it through the ceremony without her getting something on it, a rather large accomplishment for a three-year-old.

"Gabby's still getting ready and Taylor was getting restless. I told her we'd come see what her daddy was doing."

Without comment, Jax lifted her into his arms and settled her onto his hip. "Have you been helping Mommy get ready?"

Taylor nodded and proceeded to launch into all the ways she'd been helping her mother.

"I should probably get back to Gabby," Grace said. "When I left they were putting the finishing touches on her hair."

Alexander extended his hand to Grace and she took it. He pulled her close to him and whispered something in her ear. Jax didn't hear what was said, but whatever it was had Grace blushing. She nodded and walked away.

He didn't get to think about it for too long before Wes, one of his cousins, headed toward him. Jax smiled as he neared. He lowered Taylor to the ground and then embraced his cousin. "It's good to see you."

"Same here. It's been years." Three years to be more precise. When Jax had left he'd cut himself off from everyone except his parents.

He felt a tug on his pant leg and looked down. Taylor was staring up at him. "I'm gonna go help Mommy."

Jax nodded and she was off.

Wes chuckled. "She's growing up."

"Yeah."

Wes started talking about sports, always a popular subject with him. Football, basketball, hockey . . . it didn't matter. He could talk for hours and still not get tired. A half hour later, he was still standing there talking sports. He and Wes had been joined by another one of his cousins and three of his uncles. Jax wasn't a big sports fan himself, but the conversation had helped get his mind off his nerves.

His father came up beside him and clapped him on the back. "Sorry to interrupt, gentlemen, but I believe we're about ready to get this show on the road."

As soon as the words were out of his dad's mouth, all the anxiety returned.

Soft music began playing, signaling to everyone it was time to take their seats.

His dad moved to stand beside him, taking his position as Jax's best man. "Nervous?"

Jax glanced over at his father. "Is it obvious?"

Nate Brooks chuckled. "Only to those of us who've been in your shoes. You'll be fine as soon as you lay eyes on her."

Nodding, Jax took a deep breath and tried to let the music soothe him.

Several minutes passed and the song changed before he saw that flash of red again. Grace came into view, Taylor once again at her side. Bending down, Grace whispered something in his daughter's ear.

What followed had everyone cracking up. Taylor took the little basket full of rose petals she was carrying, walked about halfway down the makeshift aisle, and dumped the entire thing onto the floor. She ran back to Grace and, loud enough for the whole room to hear, asked "Did I do it right?"

Grace bit the inside of her cheek, trying not to laugh. "You did great."

She took his daughter's hand and they both made their way down the aisle to stand on the other side of the minister.

Again, they waited. Eventually the song changed, and then he saw her. All the air rushed out of his lungs as he took her in. She wore a long white dress with long sleeves and her hair was pinned up, exposing her neck. His heart pounded as she walked toward him, arm in arm with her mother.

She stopped in front of him and he didn't hesitate to grasp her hands. His father had been right.

***

99

The ceremony was short and simple. Afterward, they took a few pictures and joined their guests as they all filled their stomachs with food.

It was a great time, but by eight o'clock Jax and Gabby were both ready for some alone time. Gabby's mother, Caroline, was taking Taylor for the evening so they could be alone on their wedding night. They were all going to meet back at Jax's parents' house the next morning around ten for brunch and to open presents.

After saying goodbye to everyone and giving their daughter a lot of extra hugs and kisses since they wouldn't be there to tuck her in that night, Jax and Gabby headed back home. He parked his vehicle in the driveway and went to help his bride from the car. As soon as she was on her feet, he pressed her warm body against his and gave her a lingering kiss.

She released a sigh that sent a shot of heat straight to his groin. "We should get inside."

Gabby ran her hand down the front of his coat as she gazed up at him with a wicked gleam in her eye. "I think that's a very good idea."

He took a step back and reached for her hand, lacing their fingers together, and they made their way up the sidewalk to the front door of their home. His hands shook a little as he unlocked the door, and then turned and lifted Gabby into his arms. She didn't hesitate to wrap her arms around his neck as he carried her into the house.

Once inside, he lowered her to the floor so he could shut and lock the door. By the time he was finished, she'd already removed her coat. He quickly removed his own and put them both away in the closet.

Jax was putting the second coat on the hanger when he felt Gabby's hands on his stomach, precariously close to a part of his anatomy that was growing by the second.

"It was a lovely wedding," she said, her breath ghosting along the back of his neck.

He swallowed, trying to keep his head about him as all his blood was rushing south. "Yes, it was."

"I'm glad we didn't wait."

"So am I." He didn't dare move or he would jump her right there. Which, considering she was now his wife, wasn't out of the question, but he'd wanted something a little more romantic for their first time as husband and wife.

She ran her lips along his neck, sending shivers down his spine and making him rock hard. "I'm going to go freshen up. Can you get us a little snack? I was so busy talking to people I didn't eat all that much."

"Sure." He wondered if she heard his voice crack.

Jax felt her mouth curve into a smile. "I'll meet you in the bedroom."

Gabby moved away and he watched her disappear down the hall.

Taking several deep breaths, he tried to center himself. It was their wedding night and he wanted it to be special for her. So after putting together a plate of cheese, fruit, and crackers, along with a glass of white grape juice for both of them, he carried everything into the bedroom and began getting things ready.

He could hear her moving around in the bathroom, so he knew he had a little time. Setting the food and drinks on the nightstand, he went to the closet where he knew she had some candles. As he was pulling one off the shelf, it dropped to the floor and he bent to retrieve it.

That was when he saw a large box. It was partially open and appeared to contain books. He was about to dismiss it altogether—Gabby liked to read as much as he did—but something stopped him. Before he could think better of it, Jax flipped the cardboard flap out of the way so he could get a good look at the books inside. The four on the top were all the same. Not just the same author, but the same book. A book that he recognized.

Picking one up, he gave it a closer inspection. It was a romance novel from G. E. Lewis. The same romance novel his mother had been reading the night Jax and Gabby had come home from their date at the zoo.

G. E.

Gabrielle Elaine.

Her reaction to his mother's question about the book's author filled his memory and everything fell into place.

G. E. Lewis was Gabby. His Gabby.

He heard her enter the room and twisted, book in hand, so he could face her. All thoughts of the book he held went out the window as he took in his beautiful bride. She wore a white lace corset with white thigh-high stockings and garters. His mouth watered and kneeling instantly became uncomfortable. He stood, trying to get a little more room in his paints.

"What do you have there?" she asked as she walked farther into the room.

"What?" He blinked and followed her gaze down to the book in his hand. "Oh. I was looking for some candles and found your box of books. How come you never told me you were G. E. Lewis?"

She was in front of him and he couldn't resist touching her. Her skin was soft and smooth beneath the lace. As good as she looked in the outfit, he couldn't wait to peel it off her.

After taking the book from him, she placed it on the dresser nearby and reached for the buttons on his dress shirt. "I don't know. Maybe a part of me was worried about what you'd think if you realized what type of books I write. Especially after what your mom said." She gazed up at him. "You seemed embarrassed."

"Well, yeah. Because she's my mom. I don't want to think about my parents doing that stuff."

Gabby giggled as she popped the last button on his shirt and pushed it off his shoulders. "I see. So it doesn't embarrass you that I write sexy romance novels?" She scraped her teeth over the skin right below his collarbone and his cock twitched.

He dug his fingers into her hips and pressed her closer, letting her feel what she did to him. "Not at all. Especially if I'm the one benefiting from your creativity."

"Hmm." She hooked her finger under his belt and began backing toward the bed. "How 'bout we see how creative I can be tonight with my new husband?"

Jax lifted her up and tossed her on the bed. She landed on the mattress with a bounce.

He removed the rest of his clothes and climbed onto the bed to hover over her. "I'm all yours, wife. Let your imagination go wild."

Don't miss any Sherri Hayes news! Sign Up for Sherri's newsletter.
http://eepurl.com/J4vDb

Lieutenant Colonel Alexander Greco sat in his vehicle, staring down at the envelope in his hand. Captain Kurt Martin had given it to him eight months ago. It was a letter to Kurt's wife, Grace. Life in a combat zone was unpredictable, which Kurt knew all too well. They'd both watched too many soldiers shipped home in a body bag. Because of this, it wasn't uncommon for a soldier to make a video or write a final letter to their loved ones back home. Just in case.

Most of the time, the letter was in the soldier's personal effects. Their next of kin would discover it upon going through their loved one's things. Kurt didn't want that. He'd made Alexander promise that if anything should happen to him, Alexander would deliver the letter to Grace in person.

A chill raced down Alexander's spine as he recalled the morning that had taken Kurt's life and left Alexander with an injury that would end his military career. There had been an incident in a nearby village. They'd needed a doctor, so Alexander had loaded up his gear and joined the convoy heading out.

Everything was going as planned until they were packing up to leave. Someone yelled and then all hell broke loose. An IED exploded, sending him and several others flying. He hadn't been hurt bad from that first explosion, but it had knocked the wind out of him. Before he could get up and move, however, another explosion hit. Debris began falling from all directions. He couldn't move fast enough to get out of the way.

When the dust settled and the area secured, Alexander was pulled out of the rubble, his left leg crushed. A doctor who couldn't stand for more than an hour at a time was of no use to the Army.

Kurt hadn't been so lucky. One of the IEDs exploded right in front of him. He hadn't stood a chance.

For ten years Alexander had been an army doctor. Over that time he'd lost soldiers—men and women he considered friends. It was par for the course in a war zone. But nothing had prepared him for losing Kurt, a man he considered his brother.

Alexander closed his eyes and pinched the bridge of his nose to keep the tears at bay. Kurt was gone, along with six others in their squad.

An SUV drove past, the driver sending him a curious look. He'd been sitting in the same spot for twenty minutes with the windows rolled down letting in the breeze. Even so, the sun was beating down on his car.

Releasing a loud breath, he folded the envelope and tucked it into his shirt pocket before rolling up the windows and climbing out of the vehicle. His leg throbbed a little as he stood. He waited for it to subside as his body adjusted to the new position.

A car door slammed down the street followed by the sound of a kid laughing. Alexander shook his head, trying to clear his thoughts. After locking up the car, he crossed the street to the address he'd been given. He needed to keep his wits about him and not get distracted. He had a promise to keep.

Alexander ascended the steps of the beige two-story house. It had taken him over a month to locate Grace. By the time Alexander was released from the hospital and gotten his discharge papers, she was no longer living at the address Kurt had given him. She'd happened to mention to one of her neighbors that she was going home to be close to family. From his conversations with Kurt, he knew Grace was from St. Louis. That narrowed it down, but St. Louis was a big city. It had taken time and the help of a private investigator to finally locate her.

A wide porch ran the width of the house, but aside from an empty clay pot, it was bare. And although the yard was neat and well kept, it didn't look as if she spent much time outside. There were no flowers planted, no chairs or lawn ornaments.

He took in every detail, memorizing it. Alexander knew he was stalling. He also knew it wasn't going to get any easier the longer he put it off, and he owed it to Kurt. He'd given his word.

The sound of his knuckles against the old wood door bounced off the semi-enclosed space. He shifted his weight even though he knew it would do nothing to ebb the discomfort he was feeling. Or prepare him for facing his brother's widow.

Several minutes went by and no one came to the door. He was about to give up when he heard the sound of the deadbolt being unlocked. The door creaked open a few inches, and the small chain made a clinking sound as it moved and stretched. It was dark inside the house compared to the brightness outside, so the only thing he could see was a stray lock of blond hair.

"Can I help you?" a timid voice asked.

"Hello. I'm looking for Grace Martin. I was told she lived here." He used his most soothing doctor voice—the one he employed when he had to deliver bad news to a patient.

The woman on the other side of the door didn't respond. Maybe the private investigator had been wrong. Maybe Kurt's widow didn't live there.

"My name is Alexander Greco. I served with her husband and I was hoping to speak with her. I can come back if she's not home." His words trailed off as he heard the chain being released and the door opened wider.

"What did you say your name was again?" The woman's voice was a little stronger this time.

"Alexander Greco, ma'am. I was a doctor at the forward operating base where Grace's husband, Kurt, was stationed." He paused, his memories pulling him in a direction he didn't want to go. "We used to go on our morning runs together."

The woman opened the door wide, letting him get his first real glimpse of her. She was dressed in jeans and a faded Army T-shirt. He'd seen a picture of Kurt's wife. She was beautiful. The woman in front of him wore no makeup and had her hair pulled up in a messy ponytail. It didn't matter. Grace Martin was still stunning.

She tugged at the bottom of her shirt. "You served with Kurt." This time it wasn't a question.

"Yes, ma'am." Alexander wondered if Kurt had mentioned him to her. From the change in her features, he was assuming he had.

Grace glanced over his shoulder and furrowed her brow as though she were deep in thought. "Would you like to come in?"

"If it wouldn't be any trouble."

She stepped back, allowing him to enter.

The inside of the house was much as he imagined. She was probably renting, which explained the stark white walls and lack of pictures.

He followed her down the hallway past what looked to be a modest living room to the kitchen. It was old with laminate countertops and cabinets that looked to have been painted several times over. Along one wall was a small table with three chairs. It wasn't overly stylish, but it had a homey feel to it.

"Can I get you something to drink?" she asked.

"I'm good. Thank you."

She glanced around before lowering herself into one of the wooden chairs.

Alexander pulled out a chair and sat down, making sure not to crowd her. The last thing he wanted to do was make her feel uncomfortable. "My apologies for not calling ahead of time, but I didn't have a working phone number for you."

Grace averted her eyes and swallowed. "That's because I don't have one."

He leaned closer out of pure instinct. "You don't have a phone?"

She looked down. "Not a landline. I have a cell phone for emergencies."

Alexander relaxed a little. He knew her family was from here, but a woman living alone should at least have a phone, some way to call for help should she need it. Maybe that sounded old-fashioned, but he didn't much care. He was who he was.

A heavy silence filled the air for several moments as he searched for how to start. While Kurt had talked about his wife, Alexander didn't really know her and she didn't know him. He and Kurt had gotten to know each other during their time overseas when Kurt had been injured a few days after Alexander's arrival at the base. They'd bonded over their love of baseball and good pizza. Of course, they'd had differing opinions on both.

She met Alexander's gaze for a second, and then looked away again. "I'm okay."

The corners of his mouth lifted despite the seriousness of the situation. She obviously knew her husband well. Kurt had been a protector, just as Alexander was. It was probably another reason why they'd gotten along so well. "Kurt talked about you a lot."

Grace nodded. "He mentioned you in a couple of his emails. He said . . . he said you were a good friend."

"He was a good friend to me as well." Alexander paused. "He asked me to come see you. To find you should anything happen to him."

Alexander saw the moisture well up in her eyes and his heart broke. The urge to reach out to her was strong, but he held back. He didn't want her to be in pain, but he also knew it was inevitable. The letter Kurt asked him to deliver most likely contained his last goodbyes. Alexander didn't know how he'd handle seeing her break down in front of him, but he would do it for his friend. He owed Kurt that much.

"Were you there?" she asked, her voice barely loud enough for him to hear even sitting so close.

He felt the muscles in his throat constrict. "Yes."

She gripped the edge of the table, her fingers turning white under the pressure. "The men who came . . . they wouldn't tell me anything. Just that he . . . that he died in combat." She glanced up at him then, her eyes pleading.

As much as he didn't want to talk about that day, he would. He'd answer whatever questions she had. For Kurt. For her.

***

Grace's heart felt as if it would beat out of her chest as she waited for her guest to answer. Once his name had registered, she recalled Kurt talking about Lieutenant Colonel Alexander Greco several times. Her husband trusted him, which was what had led her to inviting him inside. If Kurt had trusted him, then she knew she could, too.

"We were in a village when we came under fire. There were explosions all around us." He paused and she held her breath waiting for him to go on. "It all happened very quickly."

Quickly. She closed her eyes as her chest constricted. It had happened quickly. He hadn't lain there and suffered. "Thank you."

The pressure of a hand on hers caused her to open her eyes. "I have something for you."

She looked at him, confused. The men who'd come to tell her that her husband had died in combat had given her Kurt's personal effects.

"Your husband gave me a letter. He asked that I deliver it personally."

Grace resisted the urge to touch her collar—the one Kurt had placed around her neck before his last deployment. It had been her only comfort the day the soldiers had knocked on her door in full dress uniform to inform her that her husband was dead. She'd lain in bed for two days before a neighbor and fellow Army wife had come to check on her. It would be so easy to sink back into that black hole. She'd been tempted several times since that day. It was only her family that had stopped her.

She'd been so lost in her thoughts, her memories, that she almost missed the envelope Alexander held in his hand. He seemed to hesitate and then held it out to her.

Reluctantly, Grace took it and placed it in her lap. With a single finger, she outlined her name written in her husband's chicken scratch. A smile tugged at her lips but was swiftly followed by a gut-wrenching ache deep in her chest. She'd always teased him about his handwriting. She'd never . . .

"Kurt asked me to make sure you weren't alone when you read it, but I can go in the other room if you'd like some privacy." His words were soft, comforting.

She shook her head, or at least she thought she did. So many emotions were rolling through her she couldn't be certain. He didn't move, though, so maybe she had.

Grace had no idea how much time had passed before she garnered the courage to pick the envelope back up and turn it over. She carefully broke the seal and removed the two sheets of paper inside. Once they were in her hands, the words staring back at her, she froze. "I can't do this."

Alexander reached out again. He grasped her free hand in his and held on tight. It was as if he could sense how much she needed his strength.

She wiped the tears from her cheeks with the back of one hand and held Alexander's fingers in a death grip with the other. He was the only thing keeping her grounded.

Her hand shook as she began to read.

> *My Grace,*
>
> *I had dreams for us. Big dreams. We were going to go on a road trip across the country and stop at all the interesting towns along the way. We were going to go on that Alaskan cruise and watch the whales playing in the bay. Hike the Grand Canyon*

and make love under the stars. So many things we wanted to do together once my tour was up.

But if you're reading this, it means we aren't going to get to do those things together and I'm sorry about that. Something has happened to prevent me from returning to you and you know that only death would keep me away. You are my heart, my soul. You are everything good and beautiful in this world, my Grace.

When I sat down to write this letter, I knew in my mind what I wanted to say, but now the words won't come. I don't want to say goodbye to you, Grace. I don't want you to have to say goodbye to me, but you have to. I know it will be difficult at first, but you are strong, Grace. You always have been.

You have to move on. You have to live.

With that in mind, I am giving you my last orders, my sweet submissive.

I want you to move back home to St. Louis. Your family is there and you will need their support. Let them love and comfort you.

I know you will need time to grieve. I want you to take that time, but I also don't want you to hide inside yourself. You have to live, remember? Make new friends, travel. Do all the things that you and I talked about doing together.

And lastly, I want you to find a new Master. I know you'll most likely go home to St. Louis, so before my deployment I did some digging and found out about a local club there called Serpent's Kiss. It's run by a woman named Katrina Mayer. I think it will be a good place for you and she can help you and make sure you find a good Dom who will take care of your needs.

I know what you're thinking, Grace, but I'm asking this of you. I'm asking you to move on. To let me go. I will always love you. Never forget that. Never doubt that. But as much as I wish it weren't so, I can't be there to care for you anymore.

Alexander is a good man. If you need anything, ask him. I have no idea if he is in the lifestyle or not, but I trust him.

Please do not mourn for me too long, my Grace. You have a lot of life left to live.

Kurt

He couldn't mean it. He couldn't.

"Grace?"

She heard someone call her name, but it sounded far away.

"Grace."

This time the voice sounded louder. Closer.

"Grace!"

A hand shook her arm, causing the letter to fall to the floor. She reached for it without checking her balance. Only a set of strong arms wrapping around her torso kept her from face-planting onto the floor.

Those same arms helped her to right herself, but all she cared about was the letter. She had to read it again. Surely she had misunderstood. She couldn't . . .

Grace scanned over the words again, but they were the same as they had been the first time. Kurt wanted her to find another Master. The rest she could do, she was already trying to do as best she could, but that? How?

Something made her look up. Alexander Greco knelt beside her on the floor, deep concern etched into his features. He must have been the one who'd called her name.

"Are you all right?" he asked.

About the Author

Sherri picked up her first romance novel when she was twelve and immediately she was hooked. She would stay up reading long after everyone else in her house had gone to bed, needing to see the hero and heroine get their happily ever after. But Sherri never imagined becoming an author.

At the age of thirty, all that changed. After getting frustrated with the direction a television show was taking two of its characters, Sherri decided to try her hand at writing an alternative ending to give the characters the happy ending they deserved.

Since then, writing has become a creative outlet that allows her to explore a wide range of emotions, while having fun taking her characters through all the twists and turns she can create.